Judas

The conflict which took place in the mind of Judas Iscariot on Palm Sunday, and during the momentous days which followed it, provides Eric Linklater with a theme of unusual and gripping interest.

Judas is represented as a wealthy young man, a member of those modernists of their time, the Sadducees. Opposed at first to the arresting of Jesus which his friends in authority demand, Judas suffers a complete change of heart after seeing Mary Magdalene washing Jesus's feet, and determines on the final betrayal.

Eric Linklater has concerned himself with character and action and with the good and bad in Judas's nature. The motives of Judas Iscariot provide an enigma of which the author's solution makes a coherent and extremely moving story.

Eric Linklater

JUDAS

A Panther Book

JUDAS

A PANTHER BOOK

First published in Great Britain by
Jonathan Cape, Ltd.

PRINTING HISTORY

Jonathan Cape Edition   published 1939
   ,,   ,,   Orkney Edition   ,,   1956
Panther Edition   published February 1959

Made and printed in Great Britain by Richmond Hill Printing Works, Limited, Bournemouth, and published by Hamilton & Co. (Stafford) Ltd., 108, Brompton Road, London, S.W.3.

CONTENTS

	PAGE
SUNDAY	7
MONDAY	24
TUESDAY	47
WEDNESDAY	73
THURSDAY	101
FRIDAY	132
SATURDAY	155

SUNDAY

1

IT was a fine cool day, but the crowd made a stinking warmth in the road through the trees. Between their green walls the air was full of a raucous noise, the day smelt of dust, the odours of sweat and foxy breath and ragged clothes. Despite this discomfort, which they made for themselves, the marching people were in holiday spirit. Many of them were shouting for war, but that was because they were so full of exultation that war to them meant immediate victory. It was excitement that made them shout, not bloody revolution.

It was their pleasure in life, even more than their strong smell, that offended Judas. He could not share it, because he could not ignore—as they did—the sweating weight of people who shambled against him, the fools hurrying behind who kicked his heels, and the yelling children who snatched from the roadway dusty palms and shook them in the clouded air. He had never had much appetite for active pleasure, and none for popular rejoicing. It was a settled state of comfort in the midst of peace that he loved above all things, and what he longed for was a double security, of body and of soul. Even now, though he had made such a fool of himself, and though his folly still held him fast, his life might be agreeable enough if civil war could be averted. If peace could be assured.

7

It was in Jericho that their danger had first become really insistent when that ruffian of a blind beggar shouted 'Jesus, Son of David, have pity on me!' Son of David! To let himself be proclaimed the Son of David when he was going to Jerusalem, where every priest and servant of the Temple, from Caiaphas to the sweepers' wives—and all the brokers and lawyers, the traders and hucksters who made their living by the Temple, and the solid thousands who found comfort in worshipping there—would see in such a claim the challenge it was, see in it rebellion, and meet it with war.

To the crowd, in their drunken joy, the penalties of revolt meant nothing. Some of them were drunk in fact as well as in fancy, for little fat Zacchaeus, his head swollen because Jesus had spent the night with him, had started the day by giving wine to anyone who wanted it. Because his house had been blessed, he said, it must be open to all. And like a fool he had given the best wine in Jericho to any lout or slattern who asked for it. So here they were, pot-valiant, shouting for war, though Jericho in all its history had never stood a siege, and its people, when they saw an enemy, stopped to look at him once only, and ran! But now, they cried, they were going to fight for the Son of David and the triumph of his Kingdom . . . In the mind of Judas a picture spread itself of frantic men, hemmed in a narrow street, their faces ridged with fear and hatred. Knives, thrust upward, slid through taut skin, through shrinking belly-wall, to find heart or lungs and release the gush of blood. He could smell the sweet hot stench of the slaughterhouse. And clubs broke matted heads, crushed bony cheeks. Men fell, clawing the wet skirts of their enemies, and were trampled underfoot. The cries of wrath turned to a shrill moan of fear, the crowd broke and ran, and there at the end of the street, a hedge of steel, was the steel discipline of Rome. A Jewish enemy stabbing them in the back, and the way closed by a Roman cohort.

Light-headed with fear, he stumbled and was caught by a grimy limping man, whose wife strode beside him, a woman tall as a camel.

'You ought to be up in front,' said the man. 'Not with all us nobodies at the back.'

"We're all equal to-day," said the woman.

In front the multitude was more orderly. The people were singing, but most of them were marching like men with a duty to perform. The nearness of their leader gladdened them, but kept them calm. Judas had been with the rest of the Twelve till the halt at Bethany, but there a well-to-do-man from Samaria, loud of voice and full of his own importance, had come ostentatiously with a present of money. The money was in a bag, denarii, shekels, didrachms, and copper coins of the Procurators, all mixed up. It amounted to so much, said the Samaritan. Judas counted it, and found it less. There was a dispute, and the Samaritan said pompously that he was not used to having his word doubted. But Judas, who kept the accounts of the Twelve with scrupulous care, was not to be cheated in such a matter, and calling witnesses, proved coldly to the Samaritan that he was wrong. The man showed his ill-humour, but tried to make a joke of the matter, saying he was pretty sure that even the lesser sum was more than anyone else had given them for a long time.

Jesus and the Disciples had not waited for him, and so thick was the crowd that Judas had no hope of rejoining them. He had fallen in with those nearest

9

him, and by chance this was the noisiest and most disorderly part of the multitude, where the Jericho men were clamouring lightheartedly for war. They were now only a mile or so from Jerusalem, and it was a realization of their nearness to the city that had suddenly made Judas weak with fear. Troops might even now be waiting for them, ready to charge and scatter this untidy and hopeless rebellion.

The crowd was increasing as it drew nearer to the walls, and the Jews of the city came out to meet it. They were as excited as the others, and the harsh noise of their jubilation reinforced the many voices that now were hoarsely failing. It had been a dry spring, and clouds of dust covered them, and coated the olive trees with double grey. A light breeze made the leaves tremble, and their silver bellies glimmered in a dusky twilight. The golden roofs of the Temple were hardly visible through the haze.

Slowly, because more and more people were coming to meet them, they went downhill. The Jews of the city, taking up the rebel cry, were hailing Jesus as the Son of David, and Judas, weak with fear, clung to the arm of the limping man and kept his place in the crowd only because he had neither strength nor the resolution to leave it.

There was a halt in front, and the many behind, pressing closer and closer together, came clumsily to a standstill. In the middle of the crowd it was almost impossible to breathe, and quite impossible to escape. Nobody knew the reason for the halt, and on all sides men were vainly thrusting against the mass in front of them, and women were screaming in sudden alarm. This, perhaps, was the end, and the soldiers were already cutting and pointing at their foremost ranks.

But then from the vanguard a shout rose, hesitant and small at first, but growing stronger as the news spread. A thousand voices repeated the story, and ten thousand cheered it. The wife of the limping man, taller than those about her, caught the tale before her neighbours, and turning, her yellow face creased with a hard delight, cried shrilly : 'Some son-of-a-bitch of a Pharisee came out and told him to stop us calling him the Son of David. But he answered, "If they stop saying it, the very stones will shout it !" And the Pharisee, the bastard, went home with his tail between his legs !'

Trembling in its immensity, like thunder directly overhead, a roar of voices cried, 'Hail ! Hail the Son of David !' Suddenly released, the great mob ran forward, staggering, tumbling in its haste. Like an avalanche, the crowded hill-side swept down against the walls, and furiously struggling the people fought their way into the city.

There were no troops to be seen, neither Romans nor soldiers of the Temple. They had either been confined to barracks or posted so discreetly as to let none be aware of their presence. Nor was there any sign of hostility among the people of Jerusalem, but they came out of their houses to see the Messiah, many cheering and all curious. Jerusalem, it appeared, was already a captured city.

2

Late that afternoon Jesus and most of the Disciples went back to Bethany. Judas made no attempt to join them, but as soon as he could, escaped from the crowd and went to his own house under the Old

11

Wall. It had been his in fact, as well as in name, since the death of his father nearly three years before. He was the only wealthy one of the Twelve, and sometimes, feeling the glow of comradeship, he had been ashamed of the gulf that riches made between him and most of his companions. At such times he had belittled his possessions, but now he was glad of them, and thankful for the barrier they reared against the stinking reckless mob in which he had been imprisoned.

He had a bath and changed his clothes. He still felt weak from the extremity of his fear, and it was an hour or two before he could persuade himself that there was no immediate danger. Then, slowly flooding in, he felt relief, and with it a soft elation that moved him to tears. Sorrow, a mild happiness, and love flowed all together through his mind. Sorrow for humanity, for the uncouth and evil-smelling people with whom he had been marching. From boyhood he had been sorry for the hideous poor of his land, but frightened of them too. Sometimes hating them, and then hating himself for permitting hatred. In the years between boyhood and youth he had often suffered an agony of detestation for his wealthy Sadducee parents and their rich friends, who openly despised the poor, and thought of them as something indifferently useful, like half-broken work-oxen; and believed that like oxen they should be kept in their own place.

In boyhood, not knowing the value of money, he had given his pennies to beggars. But then he had learnt the use of money, and perceiving that nearly everything which made his life so different from that of the beggars had been bought with money, he began to feel a passionate respect for it. He did not, like an

12

ignorant miser, love money for itself. He often spent it fairly freely on his own comfort. But he revered it for its power, and took care of all his possessions with the jealous determination of an old maid. It was only by reason of his overwhelming love that he had been able to forgive Jesus, again and again, for his carelessness about money and personal property. It worried him that a man so intellectually alert should not perceive the value of things, and he had often thought that when Jesus was destitute—as destitute he must be some day, considering the way he lived—he would bring him to stay in his own house. He would make him far more comfortable than he had ever been in his life before, and having cut him off from the other Disciples, and the heady influence of the crowds that followed him, he would persuade him to give up the political side of his teaching. If only he had forbidden the people to hail him as the Son of David. . . .

A servant came in to say that his mother wanted to know how long he was going to be. She was waiting for him on the veranda overlooking the courtyard.

With some reluctance, Judas got up. He had already had a word or two with his mother, and he knew the mood she was in. But he had been away for a long time, and he wanted to be friendly with her if he could. He was fond of her in a humiliating and unsatisfactory fashion, and often wished that he could be fond of her quite simply and whole-heartedly. He nearly always thought kindly of her when he was away from home.

'You're looking a bit better now,' she said. 'Have you had anything to eat?'

Cyborea was a tall stoutly-built woman with a broad forehead and protruding eyes. Her hair, once as red as Judas's, was now a pale sandy colour, mixed

13

with grey; but she had dark eyebrows. She had married beneath her, for Simon Iscariot, until she brought him money and influence, had had nothing to recommend him but his brains and a few poems. A lawyer without a practice, an intellectual without stability, he feared at the age of twenty-five that he had lost his way in life. But Cyborea had hardly known a doubt in all her life, and under her tuition Simon used his brains to acquire wealth and position. He had died, however, when only fifty-three, and Judas remembered him as a querulous and unhappy man.

'I suppose you realize what you've done?' said Cyborea. 'You and your Nazarene and your fishermen? It's open rebellion and nothing else. The Sanhedrin is sitting at this moment to decide what to do about it.'

'He had been led away by the people,' said Judas. 'He isn't a politician, he's a teacher, a prophet. The greatest spiritual teacher the world has ever seen. I've told you that again and again. But just recently—'

'Just recently he has proclaimed himself the Son of David, and entered Jerusalem at the head of a crowd of rebels. Are you prepared for civil war? Because that is what he means.'

'You're wrong, Mother. You misunderstand him, they all misunderstand him. War is the last thing he wants. He's a man of peace. I've heard him argue the cause of peace, and hold up the peace-maker as an example to us all. And the angel that foretold his coming promised that he would bring peace and good-will.'

Cyborea, with a movement of impatience, put down the square of coloured work she was sewing. 'Really, Judas, I don't know what to make of you!

14

The angel that foretold his coming! You, a Sadducee, to talk to me of angels! For goodness' sake leave that sort of rubbish to the Am Ha-ares, and at least think as a gentleman if you can't behave as one. It's a good thing your uncle isn't here to listen to perverted nonsense like that.'

Judas, his fingers twitching, made an effort to control himself. 'Where is he? In Rome?'

'No, he came home a month ago. He's with the Sanhedrin now. Annas asked him specially, so that he could give them advice if necessary. Annas thought his Roman connections might be useful to them.'

'Annas? But Annas has got nothing to do with the Sanhedrin. He was thrown out two years ago.'

'At a time like this we need every man who has the interest of Jerusalem at heart, and isn't afraid to speak his mind. You know what Caiaphas is like—a very agreeable figurehead, but no use in an emergency—so Annas has more-or-less been given power to take whatever measures are necessary.'

'But that's contrary to law! He's utterly unscrupulous——'

'It isn't nearly so contrary to the law as your Nazarene's rebellion, or as civil war would be.'

'For heaven's sake don't talk about war! There isn't going to be a war, and anyway I can't bear to think of it.'

'Well, you've done as much as anyone to make the danger of it real. You've got yourself to blame.'

Judas with a spasmodic movement buried his face in his hands. His hair in a bright tangle fell over his long pale fingers. As though his brains were hammering to escape, he felt a throbbing drum-beat in his head, and voices, wild and contradictory, called stupidly against each other.

His face, when he looked up, was discoloured by the pressure of his hands, and the rims of his eyes were red. Desperately he cried, 'It's all turned out so different from what I thought it was going to be! You've got to realize—it's no use your listening if you don't realize—that he's not a man like other men. He knows! I could never have followed John, and he was a saint if ever there was one. But Jesus is different. It's not only that he's good—though his goodness makes him like a flame—but he's got intellect too. He's got a brain that can loosen every knot he sees, and open every difficulty. He knows what's wrong with us all. He can drive out the poison that makes us all so miserable, and keeps the world full of fear and hatred. He's reduced all the tangle of the Law and the threat of the Commandments to two simple words: You must love God, and love your neighbour. Think what that means. It means peace and happiness for everyone. And it's peace that I want. Peace and security. I've always been afraid. When I was a little boy—that beggar at the gate into the Temple—I used to give him my pennies because I was afraid he would follow me, shuffling on his stumps, and put his black claws on me. And then I saw Jesus healing the sick, and curing the filthy deformities that people showed him. He made everybody clean, because he loved them. I couldn't do that. I've never loved anyone but him. But I loved him because I thought he could turn the world into what I want it to be. A clean and happy place. A place without fear.'

For several minutes there was silence between them. Then Judas, in the dull and heavy voice of a man tired beneath a burden, said slowly: 'It was quite true, what John said, that he wasn't even worthy to loosen his shoes. Nobody is. For Jesus is the meaning and the purpose of life, and the honour of the world.'

Again there was silence, and then Cyborea, speaking more gently than before, said with a sigh, 'I really don't know what you mean, and I can't quite believe that you do either. But that doesn't matter. What does matter is that you're in no state of mind to be mixed up with all the trouble that's coming, and what I suggest is that you should go away for a little while. Go to Egypt, for example. There's your cousin Rhoda in Alexandria, who'd be very glad to see you. And you needn't worry about things here, for your Uncle Phanuel and the Sanhedrin are quite capable of dealing with any emergency.'

Judas shook his head. 'No, I can't do that. I thought of it myself. I hate to admit it, but it's true. I've been thinking of running away for the last day or two, but I can't do it. I can't leave him.'

He got up, and walking to the end of the veranda, took softly in his hands a leafy twig of the flowering tree that grew in the courtyard. It was an old tree, unusually tall for its kind, and a branch had grown into the veranda. It was already covered with wine-pink blossom.

'It's not that I want you to go,' said Cyborea. 'You know that. I'm always so glad to have you here, though you've been a great worry to me, and still are. And it was only the other day that Tamar was saying how she wished you would come home. She's very fond of you.'

'There's more blossom than last spring,' said Judas idly.

'You weren't here last spring.'

'Well, than the year before.'

17

'Yes, that was a dreadful season. Judas, you are glad to be home again, aren't you?'

'Of course I am.'

'I hate seeing your room empty all the time.'

Judas turned suddenly, showing a frown of annoyance, and said, 'What's happened to that carpet of mine, the Ghiordes one, that used to hang there?'

'I think your sister has it in her room. She always liked it so much.'

'But she has no right to take my carpet! You know how careless she is——'

'Yes, dear, but you've been away for so long, and the carpet is far too nice to hang in a room where there's no one to look at it.'

'That doesn't matter. The carpet's mine——'

'Well, you must talk to your sister about it. I wonder where she is?'

'This isn't the first time that Tamar has taken things of mine!'

'She's like your father before we were married, poor dear. He was always thinking of something else. But shouldn't we go in now? It's getting quite cold, and it'll be dark in a minute. Dear boy, I know exactly how you feel. But don't worry, everything will be all right. Why, here's Tamar! Tamar darling, we've got Judas back. Isn't it nice to see him again?'

3

The lamps were lit, and Cyborea and her daughter sitting together. Judas had gone early to bed. Cyborea was still sewing her square of tapestry, and Tamar was embroidering a scarf. She was a tall

18

well-built girl, a year and a half older than her brother. Like him she had inherited her mother's red hair, and more of her mother's nature than Judas. She was spoiled of good looks by a rather heavy exaggeration of the same sort of features that made Judas handsome.

'He gave me back the carpet,' she said. 'He absolutely insisted on taking it, and then half an hour later brought it back, and said he was sorry for making such a fuss about nothing.'

'He can be infuriating at times.'

'He's looking terribly ill.'

'And no wonder, after the sort of life he's been leading. No proper food, and all this emotion. It's enough to upset anyone. I wish you had seen him when he arrived here! Simply on the point of collapse. It made me so angry that I tried, once again, to argue him out of all this nonsense. It didn't do any good, of course. I might have known it wouldn't. But really——'

'You weren't too hard on him, were you?'

'I told him exactly what I thought, and then he went into the most nonsensical rhapsody about this man from Nazareth, and burst into tears. So after that—oh well, I didn't say anything more. I was rather sweet to him, in fact. Or tried to be.'

'There's something quite unique about him,' said Tamar.

'About Judas? He's very clever, of course, and far too sensitive.'

'I didn't mean Judas. I meant the man from Nazareth. I saw him this afternoon.'

'You went among all those dreadful people? Tamar, you shouldn't do such things. You know that I let you have a great deal of liberty, but I do trust you to remember your position, and behave as I'd like you to.'

'It was quite all right, Mother. They were really very well behaved, especially those who were near him. He's got an amazing influence over them.'

'A man of that sort always has. The crowd will always listen to anyone who raves, and shouts at them, and promises to give them the earth.'

'But he isn't like that at all. He's quiet, and he's got a lovely voice. He was smiling, and . . . Mother, do you remember the last time Judas was here?'

'About four or five months ago? He only stayed for a night or two.'

'Yes, that was the time. Well, he was very keen that I should join them.'

'The fishermen, and the Nazarene? You join them?'

'Yes. Oh, I said it was ridiculous, of course, but he went on arguing and told me a lot about Jesus. And one of the things he said sounded so funny that I've always remembered it. Though it doesn't seem nearly so funny now that I've seen him.'

'What was it?'

'He said then that he wasn't the raving, shouting sort of revivalist that we all thought. He said, "In some of his moods, you know, he's just like one of us." '

'You mean a gentleman?'

'I suppose that's what Judas meant. Judas would never have stayed with him so long if he'd been a man like John the Baptist.'

'Well, of course he was dirty, my dear.'

'That's what I mean. It's always terribly funny to hear Judas talk about the poor and how he wants to do things for them. Because really he can't bear

20

them. He adores luxury, and if he could only stop worrying he'd be perfectly happy sitting here and admiring all his property. But I suppose he still thinks there's going to be another war.'

'There will be, unless they get hold of the Nazarene pretty soon.'

'Then Judas will go crazy. He really will, Mother. You know what he's always felt about war. And I've never been able to make up my mind whether it's really a matter of conscience, as he says it is, or simply fear.'

'Give the boy his due, my dear. He has got a conscience. He got that from his father.'

'It's been an awful trouble to him.'

'He's far too sensitive, that's all that's wrong with him. He imagines things. How he has put up with those fishermen for so long, I simply can't think. I should have thought he was the last person on earth to endure discomfort. And yet all this time he's been going about the country, playing at being poor, and seemingly quite determined about it. But you can't imagine him being really poor, can you?'

'It would kill him. He does love to own things. That carpet, for instance.'

'Poor Judas, we mustn't be too censorious.'

'I'm terribly fond of him, but he did make me angry about the carpet. And I was so glad to see him.'

'You behaved very nicely to him.'

'Mother, don't you think that if anyone owns a lot of property he ought to be prepared to defend it?'

'Well, everybody is, I should think. Nobody I ever knew would let anyone take anything from him without creating a great deal of trouble.'

'But Judas isn't like that. He's a pacifist because

he wants to own his property in perfect safety. Yes, I know he's got a conscience, but he's also got a good idea of what would be useful to him.'

'You're being too theoretical now . . . Where are you going?'

'I want some more silk.'

'What colour is it?'

'Blue.'

'Won't this do? It's the same shade, isn't it?'

'I'm not sure. It's difficult to tell by lamplight. Oh, it doesn't matter. I've done enough for to-night.'

'You must be tired, after walking about all afternoon. You had better have a glass of wine, or would you like some hot milk?'

'No, I don't want anything.'

'Judas hasn't been trying again to persuade you to join the Nazarene, has he?'

'No, Mother.'

'You'll tell me if he does?'

'There's really no danger.'

'The men are bad enough, but some of the women who follow him are simply scandalous.'

'You mean Mary of Magdala?'

'She's the most notorious, but I'm told there are others of the same sort.'

'She was there to-day. She's perfectly lovely.'

'She certainly was ten years ago.'

'I heard some people saying that she had paid for their last journey to Galilee.'

'I imagine she could easily afford it.'

'But where did she get all her money?'

'Some of it from your Uncle Phanuel, my dear. He kept her at one time, till she nearly ruined him.'

'There's one thing to be thankful for: I don't suppose Judas has had much to do with her.'

'No. Judas has never given me any trouble that way. Well, I'm going to bed.'

'I'm going too. Good-night, Mother.'

'Good-night, my dear. Sleep well. You're not worrying, are you? I'm perfectly confident, though I wish Phanuel had come to tell us what the Sanhedrin has decided to do. Still, we can rely on them absolutely now that Annas has gone back. I was so relieved when I heard that that silly man Caiaphas wasn't going to be left in charge. Well, good-night, dear. Give me a kiss.'

'Good-night, Mother.'

MONDAY

1

BEFORE it was light Judas got up and left the house and went out of the city. He had slept well, and waking with new confidence put away the memories of yesterday with loathing. He had been guilty, once again, of letting his belief grow weak and falter: that was what had been wrong with him. Nothing but lack of faith. And how ridiculous it was to have been afraid, of war, of anything at all, when he knew that in Jesus was the safety of all mankind. But he felt better now. He felt strong, and almost brave, for now his faith was whole and perfect.

The morning came like a spray of cool water. The light was crystal, the air brisk and clean. A little breeze made the olive trees twinkle, and scatter silver streaks among the shadow of their branches. Then the air grew warm, and before he had climbed the hill the sun was above its crest, and dazzling his eyes. He looked down at the city, at the darkness of its valleys, and precipitous walls. At the enormous Temple, white as snow and crowned, before the rising sun, with the heavy splendour of burning gold. It was a sign of more than spiritual authority. It was temporal power, and had in its service cruelty and cunning and great wealth.

But he had no fear now, neither of the Temple nor its allies. He had made submission, and opened

24

his heart to a faith as incurious and absolute as that of a child. He was very happy that he had been able to do this.

For a little while he sat among the olive trees, looking down at the road to Bethany. And presently he saw them coming.

There was a crowd of people in formation like a shoal of little fish in a stream, when the current shapes their mass. They were coming slowly, with a wavering flux in their movement, as though swimming against the invisible current. And then from the slope of the hill, from hollows and couches among the rocks, rose another crowd and ran to meet them. Thousands of people had been waiting there all night, wrapped in their cloaks, or cold in their rags. They got up shouting, their garments large and loose, and hurried pell-mell down the side of the hill. Judas was startled by the suddenness of their appearance and the wild rapidity of their movement. They were like a flock of birds—crows rising, harsh of voice, with ragged wings—and in the fixity of their expression was something of the mindless intensity of birds. He followed them, his heart beating more quickly, his breath coming fast and shallow.

The people from Bethany were brought to a halt when the second crowd met them. The new-comers clustered round the vanguard of the marchers, where Jesus was walking with some of the Twelve, and would not let him go. For a long time there was confusion. Then slowly, as if a stubborn purpose were showing itself, the march was resumed and the thickened crowd went on towards the city.

From an outcrop of rock in the shoulder of the hill Judas looked down and saw Jesus clearly. He experienced an emotion such as he had known perhaps half a dozen times before. A flood of joy, crying aloud to be spent, was released in him. He felt limp, as though the solid stiffness of his body had broken down, and through its opening channels a glad assurance was running softly out. He gave himself up entirely to the virtue that could so strongly draw happiness from its dark confinement, and with odd humility, with gaiety of spirit yet more unusual, he joined the nearest section of the crowd and turned with them toward Jerusalem.

There was much loud excitement, and many, with trembling lip and burning eye, were in a state of exaltation. Others were laughing and exchanging with cheerful irrelevance their usual scraps of trumpery gossip. Here and there were men like oxen in the butcher's yard, men who had no idea of what was happening, nor seemed to care; but feeling the drag of companionship, went marching because others did. They stared in sullen bewilderment at their noisier fellows and sometimes, to prove themselves, let out a bellow of dubious laughter. But others, and many others, were eager, practical, and alert. They knew what they wanted, and some were roughly sure of getting it.

A tall sturdy man, who by his smell was a tanner, was saying, 'It's the poor man's turn to-day, and by God we'll take it. Roman or Sadducee, Greek or the bastards of them all—it doesn't make a penn'orth of difference to us what they call themselves. If a man's rich, he's an enemy. If he's poor, he's a friend. That's the only difference to-day.'

'And to-morrow there won't be any difference at all, because there won't be any rich left.'

'There won't be any poor either.'

'That's right, there won't be any poor.'

An old man, tall and thin, his eyes on some remote distance, his face burnt by the desert and seamed with an old wound, was chanting: 'The sword of Gideon, the sword of Gideon! He shall save Israel from the hand of the Midianites!'

'What in hell have the Midianites got to do with it?'

'Don't you worry about the sword of Gideon, Uncle. It's a man of peace that's leading us now.'

'A man of peace!' exclaimed the tanner. 'What's the good of peace? Nobody ever got anything without fighting for it, and we won't either.'

'You trust him, he'll know the way.'

'There's only one way.'

'Don't you believe it. He'll show you something that no one's ever thought of.'

'And that's the poor having a good time—but not till we cut a few throats first.'

'They can keep their throats, all I want's to get a knife in their money-bags.

A genial stout little man, puffing as he walked, said to Judas, 'And what do you think is going to happen? You ought to have a better idea than most of us.'

'I don't know,' said Judas. 'It will be as he decides.'

He had heard the surrounding chatter without really listening to what was said. He was still conscious of an extraordinary lightness of spirit, a buoyancy that seemed to carry his body with it. He stumbled occasionally, but without annoyance, and with the thoughtless recovery of a drunk man. 'I don't know,' he repeated, 'but everything will be all right. We can leave it to him.'

The old man, desert-burnt, looked round and said

27

in the voice of exaltation, 'Last night I laid a sheep-skin on the ground, and this morning all the grass was dry, but the fleece was wet with dew. I wrung from it a full bowl of water. God's mercy will be upon us, measure-full and overflowing.'

'The Kingdom of God!'

'And no more clanking bloody Romans in Judea!'

'There's no harm in a Roman if he isn't rich. Can't you get the idea of that into your thick head? It's the system that's wrong, not the poor bastards that work it.'

'Well, we'll see soon enough.'

'Yes, we'll soon see. You can leave it to him, he'll know what to do.'

'He'll know what to do, he's the poor man's friend.'

'The poor man's friend!'

2

The crowd that had gathered about Jesus did not seem to have lessened the number of people in the outer court of the Temple. In that huge area, enclosed on three sides by decorated colonnades, on the fourth by the heavy white-and-gold mass of the Temple buildings, was the population of a small town; and like the population of any town it was busy with buying and selling. Much of the trading was in sheep and oxen, and the stench of a cattle-market blew strangely through arcades that were roofed with elaborate cedar and walled with Corinthian columns. Money-changers, piemen, dealers in oil and incense and souvenirs of Jerusalem, had their stalls in this environment of splendour, so that when they raised their eyes—exclaiming with fury at their imminent ruin—it was to see an acanthus-forest of glittering brass; and when they turned aside to spit, they discharged their rheum on a sea-green or golden-branching marble floor.

There was, at the moment, rather a shortage of animals, and prices were high. For a sacrificial ox or lamb they were asking more than double its ordinary value, and a pair of doves, the poor man's offering, cost as much as would buy a dozen in better times. The money-changers, to do business at all, had been forced to lower the rate of exchange—from other coinage into Temple currency—and were unusually ill-humoured. Most of them had their tables in the western colonnade, south of the Gate of Coponius; and from early morning there had been a good deal of anger and altercation there. Ill-temper and the dubious honesty of a Temple official had also provoked a dispute that now gathered, in the middle of the Court of the Gentiles, a crowd of several hundred people.

A man from Beth-hoglah, in the Jordan valley, coming with most of his family and many of his dependants, had brought his own sacrificial animals, half a dozen young bulls and a score of lambs. The Temple official had refused to pass them. They were, he said, all blemished in one way or another. The man from Beth-hoglah would have to buy others. But this he refused, maintaining that his own beasts were as whole and clean as any to be found; and all his relations and servants began to exclaim against injustice, and to call the attention of the gathering onlookers to the excellence of their cattle, the shapeliness of their lambs. Dealers intervened, eager to sell their certified animals. They shouted, pulled a heifer and a couple of frightened sheep into the circle, and tugged, one against another, at the garments of the stubborn man from Beth-hoglah. He, paying no attention to them, was arguing with a couple of angry priests. The crowd grew, and a woman with a high tearing voice began to scream.

The plaint of sheep mingled with the roar of human voices. The lowing of cattle echoed through the colonnades. Wisps of yellow straw blew hither and thither, children ran to and fro. An old man, oblivious of all but his own need, was gathering dung for fuel, and a scarecrow fellow from the desert of Jeruel leant against a Corinthian column chewing melon-seeds. The clink of money sounded briskly in the western colonnade.

It was through the Shushan Gate, in Solomon's Porch, that Jesus entered. The multitude that followed him flowed forward on either side like the horns of a crescent. They were quiet now, and he walked in the gulf of their breathless expectancy. As though it were being swept away by a broom, the ragged din of voices died gradually before them, till in half the great court there was no longer any noise of human kind except the shuffling of many feet. The bleating of a sheep sounded as clear and lonely as on a mountain-side. But on the people a silence lay as if it were the dead hours of the night. And as if waking in the night to find an angel or a murderer by their bed, they waited in a still fear.

There was a group before him, of priests fat with extortion and dealers wrath-red with greed and shouting for their price. He spoke to them, and his voice drove the blood from their cheeks: 'Is it not written that my house shall be called a house of prayer for all nations? But you have made it a den of robbers.'

None had heard him speak in such a voice before; nor any other man. It was the voice of war. It was the trumpets when the line of spearmen has broken and the enemy's horsemen gather their reins for the charge. When the knees of the horses are like a breaking wave, and the ground thunders, and the trumpets cry. In all who heard it, their blood grew faint and their legs reluctant.

To Judas the voice was like a draught of wind that carried him skyward to an altitude where the air was cold and thin. Fear assailed him, and a rocking vertigo, as though he had been set upon a rock that overhung a cloudy precipice, and the village below, moving in the drifting cloud, was minified to a dreadful unreality. His stomach rose, and he knew that he could not live at such a height. His late-found confidence fell from him, a shrivelled thing, and the strength of the morning failed him. He yearned for the easy comfort of the valley below. He longed for rest. From conscience, as from fear; from the intolerable light of such a vision, as from the stricken multitude before him, he begged for release.

Slowly the crowd retreated. They hauled their cattle from the wooden pens beneath the colonnade, and drove their lambs between the feet of frightened people. From the gateways ran jerkily, like water leaping from a skin, knots and clusters of men and women, fearful of a wrath whose fuller manifestation they could not imagine.

In the western colonnade the money-changers stood by their tables. One of them, gross of figure and of face, full-bearded, found his tongue and thickly shouted his defiance and protest. The voice answered him, and his quarrel crumpled like a man falling beneath a sword. Then suddenly came the crash of a table overturned, the silver chink and chattering of money scattered about the pavement. From the crowd rose a murmur of delighted horror. Here and there someone made a protesting movement, but with a guilty look at his neighbours checked himself in time. The money-changers, retreating like brutes before the whip, cried harshly in the agony of their loss, but dared not make a move to save their property.

Judas felt the blood come heavily to his temples. This was no vision of ineffable majesty, but power reduced by action to a human dimension. And in such a scale it seemed mere wantonness, the meaningless destruction of all that made the daily business of living comprehensible . . . The matter of money was to Judas his familiar territory. For years he had helped his father in the management of his property; taken his rents and calculated interest; made payment for service and stored receipts. He had looked after the accounts of the Twelve with exact and unremitting care. Money was the fruit of labour and the harvest of long thought, a coat against winter and bread in the mouth of the hungry. His anger rose like the smoke of a new-made fire, and against this scene of waste and ruin his thoughts ran with murderous feet. But the fear that held back the crowd and drove the money-changers before it, held him also in fetters, and his anger piled itself against a wall of impotence.

Rolling edgeways, a little procession of silver coins came uncertainly towards him. He bent instinctively to pick them up, and turning against the crowd began to force his way through it. He pushed them apart and drove his trembling body to the outer skirts of the multitude, and still in a hurry left the Temple by one of the weasel-gates in the Royal Porch. This was the gate, he remembered, where the legless beggar had been used to sit, whose dark talon-hands had frightened his dreams in boyhood. But the beggar had been dead for years, and a naked boy, with lolling head and a body that never stopped shaking, sat there in his place.

Walking quickly, as if he hoped that by violent movement he could dislodge the burden on his mind, he went through the city and came to his own house. He saw no one but a servant or two, and in his room lay down and let the rival armies trample his mind. Faith charged, and was repelled by intolerable facts. All that his body loved rose in the stirrups and fought with that in which, while the morning shone, his spirit had so joyously believed. There was no peace to be found in such a battle, and by-and-by exhausted, he fell into a troubled sleep.

When he woke up his right hand was cold and cramped. He found that his fingers were still clenched over the couple of shekels he had picked up in the Temple.

3

Uncle Phanuel was a heavily-built man with a roughish red face, with drooping eyelids, drooping pouches beneath, and a little sagging of the cheeks into a thick neck. He was clean-shaven in the Roman style, but his beard grew high, and over his cheek-bones ran a dark pilous ridge. His hair had once been as brightly black as his sister's was red; but now, when hers was faded, his was blacker still, for it was carefully dyed. His voice was good-humoured, with the tone of well-fed arrogance.

He had been talking to Cyborea about Judas.

'There's no use your trying to make him see reason,' she said. 'He could see it perfectly well if he liked, but he simply doesn't want to.'

'It was my idea to make him want to.'

'You can't do it, Phanuel. You may drive him into a corner, but he'll jump out of it in a fit of exaltation. He's like his friend from Nazareth : he works miracles now.'

'He must have changed a lot. There used to be a great deal of common sense in the boy. Oh, I know he's always been a bit temperamental, but that's largely because he isn't quite up to the weight he carries. He's too clever for his years, and perhaps a bit too thoughtful. But there's sound stuff in him. He's got an uncommonly good notion of business, and except when he's riding one of his hobbies, he shows a remarkable grasp of argument. I feel perfectly sure that he won't ignore an appeal to common sense.'

'You don't know him as well as I do. I love him—'

'Well, naturally.'

'Yes. He's my only son. But sometimes he angers me beyond endurance, and the reason for that is that he hasn't got any common sense. He's clever, yes. More than clever enough to understand business. But he's divided against himself, and because of that he's unpredictable. For example : he's been talking for years, in a way I've never heard before, about *peace*. According to him it's a moral necessity. And now he's in league with this man who's trying to stir up civil war! And what makes it doubly infuriating is that Judas is still at heart a pacifist.

34

He told me so himself. It isn't only that he likes the idea of peace, but he's dependent on it. He's that sort of boy.'

'Well, I've no quarrel with him there. I'm a pacifist myself. We're all pacifists nowadays. What would happen to my business if there was any trouble with Rome? What would happen to your investments? I'm as much in favour of peace as Judas is. More, I dare say. And if you'll let me talk to the boy——'

'You won't make him more miserable than he is already?'

'I'm going to help him, if I can. After all, he's my nephew as well as your son.'

'If his father had been alive——'

'My dear Cyborea, you know perfectly well that Simon's way of dealing with any personal difficulty was to avoid it. Simon wouldn't have been a scrap of use.'

'Sometimes, I think, his brain used to work in the same way as Judas's. He used to say odd things, and I never quite knew whether he thought that everybody else was a knave, and merely that he himself was a fool. Though he wasn't, of course. As a young man he was perfectly brilliant.'

'Now go and get Judas, please. I haven't a great deal of time, and there's a definite proposal that I want to put to him. A proposal that may go a long way to solving his difficulties.'

Phanuel got up and walked heavily to the corner of the veranda which the flowering tree invaded. Idly he took hold of the branch, and stared, frowning at its blossom.

Quiet of foot, Judas came and greeted him: 'Mother told me you were here.'

'My dear boy! I'm so glad to see you!'

35

Phanuel's voice was warm and friendly. There was a protective quality in it, and while he spoke, of lively commonplace and the trivialities of family affairs, the rind of lonely perplexity that imprisoned Judas was softened a little. His manner grew slightly easier.

'And Tamar, so your mother was telling me, has followed the fashion and been to hear this Nazarene friend of yours. What did she think of him?'

'She didn't say very much.'

'Well, you know him better than most people, of course. I don't suppose her opinion would have been of any interest to you. He's a very remarkable man, Judas.'

'Yes, very.'

'I've been sitting with a special committee of the Sanhedrin—there was a meeting last night and another to-day—and I don't suppose I'm telling secrets when I say that this friend of yours was the principal topic of discussion. We're very much interested in him, and personally I'd like to meet him. From all I've heard he's a man with an uncommonly good brain.'

'Is it true that Annas is in power again?'

'It's not an official appointment, but he has been sitting with us as a sort of special adviser.'

'He has no right to be there. He was deposed a couple of years ago for maladministration of Temple funds——'

'Yes, it was a very unsavoury case. But really it was a technical offence, and in view of the special circumstances to-day I think we were justified in asking him to help us. He's a very able man, he knows his own mind, and he's a good Sadducee.'

'Is flagrant dishonesty consistent with being a good Sadducee?'

Phanuel made an angry movement, but checked himself, and very gravely said, 'I know for a certainty that Annas most bitterly regrets the mistake he made, and if he was really to blame—which to my mind is still doubtful—you can depend on it that he'll do all he can to make amends. None of us is perfect, and I for one am glad to show, by willing association with him, that I am perfectly ready to forgive and forget. Especially at a time like this, when a man like Annas, with a constructive brain and a good understanding, is really indispensable.'

'What is the Sanhedrin going to do?'

'We haven't come to a decision. As a matter of fact, they were unanimous in refusing to come to a decision until I had consulted you.'

'Me! What have I got to do with them?'

'You're in the unique position of being the only man with brains, the only man with a sense of social responsibility, who has been in close contact with Jesus almost from the beginning of his campaign. You can give us better information than anybody else, and quite frankly we're in need of information. Now don't misunderstand me: I'm not trying to undermine your allegiance. I know that you're with him, heart and soul . . .'

Phanuel paused. Judas, with a downward movement of his head, had clasped his hands together till the knuckles shone white.

'We realize,' Phanuel continued, 'that your loyalty to him, your personal loyalty, is unshakable.'

'I love him.'

'That I can well understand. The Church to-day

is in sore need of such a man. Annas himself—Annas whom you so much dislike—spoke very favourably about some of his teaching. But what we cannot discover is his precise and whole intention.'

'He has come to preach the Kingdom of Heaven. He said himself that his purpose was not to destroy the Law and the prophets, but to fulfil them.'

'Now there is a difficulty to begin with. The teaching of some of the prophets, though admirable in their own time, would have very disastrous consequences to-day. This business of Jewish nationalism, for example. I dare say you could find a good deal of backing for it in the prophets, but if you put it into practice it would simply mean a silly little war against Rome, and our immediate extinction.'

'But his purpose isn't war. He's a man of peace.'

'Then I must protest that his notion of peace appears to be rather different from that of most people. But let that pass. I want you to listen to this, and tell me what you think of it as a reading of the situation. The programme of this Nazarene Jesus—this man of great ability and the most impeccable ideals—can be divided into three parts. In the first place, he evidently wants to reform the Church.'

'He wants to re-fashion the hearts and minds of men.'

'Well, surely that is a matter for the Church? Let's keep the issue as clear as possible, and say that his first intention is the reform of our religious institutions. In the second place, he has identified himself with a social movement. He has allowed himself to be represented as a champion of the poor, of the depressed classes. And thirdly, it is the opinion of most of my colleagues that he is in favour of Jewish nationalism. Now what do you say to all that?'

'You can't describe his mission in ordinary terms. It's the Kingdom of Heaven that he preaches, and all our politics have no meaning in such a scale as his. Nations mean nothing to him, and the poor aren't sacred to him because they are poor, but because they can be saved. I remember him once saying that God makes the sun rise on the evil and the good alike, and sends rain for the just and the unjust. For they can all believe, they can all be cured of their sin and their follies. They can be made perfect, if only they believe in him and love him. Don't you see how simple everything is, if you look at it from his point of view? If we could love God and our fellow-men, if we behaved to everyone with loving consideration, then to all intents the Kingdom of Heaven would be here and now. And that's the object of his teaching.'

'I see,' said Phanuel and, to avoid the embarrassment of looking at Judas, considered his finger-nails. 'I see,' he repeated, slowly and reflectively. 'Yes, perhaps I was taking too narrow a view. But tell me, do you yourself find the problem simple? You say that Jesus does. Now is that your opinion too?'

Judas hesitated, caught his breath, and hoarsely muttered, 'No!'

'No, I didn't expect it to be. There are obvious difficulties in the way of translating this idealistic vision—I've nothing but sympathy for it myself—into practical terms. A lot of difficulties. And a man like you, with your training and upbringing and sound common sense, must be acutely aware of such difficulties. And so we come to the methods by which your leader hopes to effect this transformation—is that too strong a word? No, I don't think so—this transformation of the world. His methods. They're various, of course. Now do you find yourself in equal sympathy with all his methods?'

'You mustn't ask me to criticize him.'

'No? I've always thought that helpful criticism was one of the privileges of friendship.'

'Not in this case.'

'Well, you know best, of course. But if I put it another way, if I were to ask: What, in your opinion, is the most valuable feature of his ministry? Could you answer that?'

'Why, he is. He himself. He's the very heart of his teaching.'

'Now we're getting somewhere. Now I can help you, I think, and help him too. But you must prepare yourself for a shock.'

'I'm getting used to shocks.'

'Yes, poor fellow. All this must have been very trying for you; although you must have been comforted, of course, by your conviction that in all essential matters Jesus is in the right . . . Well, without more ado, the position is that a very influential body of opinion in the Sanhedrin is in favour of immediately arresting him and charging him with high treason.'

'But there's no case against him!'

'Our friends the Pharisees, and our temporary allies the Herodians, seem to think there is.'

'But you don't agree with them! And Annas——'

'To Annas and Caiaphas and myself, and to the other Sadducees on the committee—that is to say, to the most reasonable and responsible members of the government—the situation does not as yet call for extreme measures. But what we are all agreed on is that the interests of the State are paramount, and that we have, now and always, the fullest justifi-

40

cation for taking any action necessary to secure it. To us, the Sadducee members, it seems that public safety could best be secured, and the person of Jesus himself respected, by taking him into protective custody.'

'You mean, to arrest him?'

'No. Not in the criminal sense of the word. But for his own benefit, as well as the protection of other people's lives and property, we think that his liberty should be restricted for a little while.'

'But the people wouldn't let you arrest him. They would riot, there would be civil war at once!'

'We have foreseen that danger, and frankly I hope that you will help us to avert it. If you could persuade him that it would be in his own interest, and eventually in the interest of his mission, to submit to a period of detention; or, failing that, if you could arrange that he should be alone with you, in some unfrequented place——'

'Oh, that's damnable!'

'It would be entirely for his own good.'

'That I should betray him?'

'I would rather put it, that you should save him from the consequences of his present line of action. Think it over, my boy. Think very carefully before you refuse.'

'There's no need for me to think. You ask me to commit the most damnable treachery, and then suggest that I need time to consider my answer! My answer's no! And ten years from now it will be the same!'

'Yes, that is what I expected you to say. But second thoughts have often a great deal to be said for them, you know. I'm older than you, my dear boy. I've seen rather more of the world, and I'm your friend. Take it from me that what I suggest is not only for the general welfare of our country, but for the welfare of your friend from Nazareth. So think it over, and let me know to-morrow, as early as you can, if your second thoughts are different from your first.'

4

The taverns and the streets of Jerusalem were full of excited people. In the darkness they went to and fro, came clattering down hilly lanes, and in a broader thoroughfare spilt their company against a more numerous and slow-moving mass. To everybody it seemed that something of great importance was bound to happen soon; but nobody could in the least imagine what it would be. Some argued, theorized, or dogmatically explained what should be done; but most were satisfied with occasional shouting and the vague anticipation of seeing their enemies humiliated. Some declared their eagerness to fight— for a cause they could not wholly or satisfactory define —but more believed in the miracle of a bloodless achievement of all they desired. Here and there a Zealot, under the light of a smoky torch, made inflammatory speeches. The people listened for a while, and cheered him; but then moved away to exchange encouraging remarks with friendly strangers, or embrace, in sudden kindness, their chance-met neighbours. The threat of wholesale riot was overlaid by this warm and general display of friendliness. The crowds were still good-humoured, and as yet there had been no show of violence.

Tavern-keepers did a roaring trade, and every inn

was full. The tanner who had come from Bethany that morning, and whose talk had been all of fighting and the rights of the poor, had a sister who was a servant in a small inn by the Bethlehem road. He sat there with his friends about him : a pedlar called Simon; a long-faced fellow with a great hook-nose, by name Cushi; and the little plump good-natured man—he was half a Greek, his name was Amplias —who had talked with Judas on the road. Zadok, the old man with the desert-burnt face and a mind bewildered by the desert, had fallen asleep, and beneath the weight of his nodding head his beard lay crumpled on his chest.

The tanner still spoke of war. He thought the time had come when all the poor men of the world, having realized their innumerable strength, were about to seize the comfort and the wealth that rich men pretended were theirs alone. He had a rope round his waist, and was ready, so he boasted, to play hangman to every usurer, capitalist, or plutocrat they caught. But Simon the pedlar had no great opinion of the poor, neither of their courage nor their cleverness. Only by a miracle, he said, would they ever get what they wanted, and that was why he followed Jesus, who, if he cared, could turn the rich into swine and drive them over a cliff; and shake a thousand shekels out of his sleeve for every poor man in Judea.

'And would that,' asked Amplias, 'create the Kingdom of Heaven?'

'It would be a lot liker heaven than the hell we're living in now,' said the tanner.

'We've got to get rid of the Romans first,' said Cushi. 'We've got to drive those square-faced bastards into the sea before we can do anything else.'

'If I've told you once,' shouted the tanner, 'I've told you a hundred times that a Roman soldier's a poor bloody fool like yourself, and what we've got to do is to make common cause with him against the officer-class, and the international class of pluto-crats that's exploiting both him and us.'

'A Roman's a Roman, whether he's a lousy private or a stinking general. And I don't like them.'

'Do the Romans want to make common cause with us?' asked Amplias.

'Some of them do, and we've got to educate the others.'

'That would be a hell of a miracle,' said Simon.

A tall and burly man, much better dressed than those about him, rose from a neighbouring group, and staggering slightly caught Amplias by the shoulder. 'Bad wine,' he exclaimed. 'I've been drink-ing a lot of damned bad wine. Look here, d'you know what happened to me this morning? Well, let's have another drink, and I'll tell you all about it. It's a typical story.'

He sat down, and after calling loudly for wine, looked solemnly at his new companions, and said: 'We're all friends here. I can tell that by the look of you. I can read character like a hawk, and as soon as I saw that cross-eyed sniffling snuffling priest this morning, I said to myself, He's a crook! And so he was. Well, here's to the Nazarene, and good luck to him! I've been drinking his health all day. I've lost all my friends, and found new ones where-ever I go. It's a great life, men, and the Nazarene's a man after my own heart. Fill 'em up, there's plenty more where that came from.'

His noise woke the old man Zadok, who opened his rheumy eyes and said in a faint but solemn voice,

'Look not upon the wine. At the last it shall bite like a serpent and sting like adders.'

'It's all right,' muttered the tanner. 'He's a bit queer. He thinks we're going to have trouble with the Midianites.'

'I've been dealing with worse than Midianites,' shouted the new-comer. 'I've been dealing with a gang of sneak-thieves and blackmailers. Now you listen to me. I come from Beth-hoglah, in the valley of the Jordan, and I went to the Temple this morning with my wife and my two sons, and their wives, and Sarah my youngest daughter, and Jonah my head cattleman, and—well, there were about twenty of us altogether. I don't know how many. But we had our own animals, and every one of them I'd chosen myself. They were the pick of the flock, the pick of the herd. And what d'you think that scab of a squint-eyed priest said about them . . .'

'You're right,' said the tanner, when at last the long story was finished. 'It's blackmail, and nothing else. The whole system's built on blackmail and daylight robbery.'

'But it didn't work this time,' said the man from Beth-hoglah. 'The Nazarene came along and drove 'em out of the Temple like a boy scaring crows. Laugh! I've been laughing ever since. But I'm serious too. Don't think I'm not serious! From now henceforward I'm with the Nazarene heart and soul.'

'We're all with him,' said Simon the pedlar.

'To-morrow,' said Cushi, 'we'll see him driving the Romans out of Judea just like he drove the priests out of the Temple.'

'I'll take you six to one that he does nothing of the sort!' exclaimed the tanner.

'What's your opinion?' asked the man from Beth-hoglah, and thrust his now solemn and glistening face to within a couple of inches of Amplias.

'I really don't know,' said Amplias. 'I suppose we've just got to wait and see what happens. But whatever it is, I wouldn't miss it for anything. We're going to make history within the next day or two, that's certain. It's a wonderful age we're living in, because events are moving so fast. Faster than they've ever moved before.'

Zadok, half asleep again, his breath blowing apart the hairs of his beard, whispered, 'The people are too many. Gideon sent away all his army but three hundred. And with three companies, of a hundred men in each, he made slaughter of the Midianites.'

TUESDAY

1

HE must tell Jesus of the new danger that threatened him. He must warn him that he was likely to be arrested, and persuade him to flee into the hills, to Galilee again, somewhere far from Jerusalem and the prison of the Sanhedrin . . .

Like the squealing hinges of a door that is forever opening into a room where a man sits, wishing only for quiet, the urgency of saving Jesus from his enemies had come with strident reiteration to Judas's inner ear through the long hours he lay sleepless on his bed. He had tried to ignore it. He had tried to persuade himself that he and all the Disciples, and Jesus himself, were now in a tide of events that must flow, moon-bidden, in their destined course. He had no power to stop or hinder the irresistible stream that carried them forward. They must swim with the current and take their chance like a rudderless boat . . . But the door opened and the hinges cried : You can warn him now, before it is too late. You are one of his company and loyalty binds you, honour is compulsive, and because in your own mind you know that he is right, you must take no thought of danger to yourself, but think only of saving him.

It would be perilous, he knew, to tell Jesus of what was being plotted against him. If he and his Disciples were suddenly to escape from Jerusalem, the Sanhedrin would know at once who had given them warning of its plans, and its anger would fall terribly on the informer. He now stood as near to danger as Jesus himself—and who was he to dare the immemorial strength of the priests and the Roman guardians of law? He could do no good . . .

Again the door opened. He pulled a blanket over his head, but could not keep out the cry of his conscience, turning on its hinges.

At last, when the darkness was growing pale, he got up and dressed himself, moving tip-toe and with trembling fingers, like a boy who has nerved himself to go out and climb a forbidden cliff.

The morning air was cold. He breathed it with a gasp, as though it were a cup of icy water, and his stomach contracted. He gathered his cloak more tightly round him, and with clumsy fingers opened the narrow outer door that led into a cobbled lane. He had gone a few yards when suddenly he stopped, and turned again.

Beside the door there was a niche in the wall, where every morning a servant put a basket of crusts and remnant meat for beggars. Half-consciously Judas had glanced at it, and a moment later it occurred to him that the basket was unusually full. He went back and found in it, as well as scraps of bread and a bowl of porridge, three barley loaves, a piece of good meat, and a couple of dried fish. A little jet of anger leapt in his mind. There was no possible excuse for such a waste of food. It was good food, food that anyone might be glad to eat, and it was being thrown away. Food that had been bought with his money.

He took a loaf in his hand. It was a little hard, but there was nothing wrong with it. His anger grew and took possession of him. Anger against the sin of waste. This idiot-squandering must have been going on for months. All the time he was away, all the weeks of his self-denial and hardship and righteousness, there had been this daily waste of food, because servants, with none to watch them, could show their malignancy, their hatred of those who paid them, by destroying their property. All that he valued, all that he had worked for, was being devoured and corrupted. His peace was threatened, his goods were being thrown away. He felt the waste of a few loaves and two little fishes as though it were a cancer gnawing him; and pushing open the narrow door he strode into the courtyard and shouted harshly for Barak the steward.

'Look!' he exclaimed. 'Look at this loaf! I found it in the beggars' basket, and there are two others there as well. Whole loaves being thrown away, and good fish and meat!'

Barak was a little round man, pot-bellied, with twinkling black eyes and a loose mouth. 'They're stale,' he said, 'and I expect the fish had gone a bit bad, sir. In this weather——'

'It's all perfectly good food. I smelt it.'

'Well, sir, in a house as big as this there's always bound to be a certain amount of waste——'

'Waste! That's what I'm complaining of. Don't you see that it's wrong to waste things? It's morally wrong, socially wrong, wrong in every way. There's no excuse for it.'

'But the food isn't exactly being thrown away sir. I mean, it's always eaten. There's plenty of poor people.'

'I know that as well as you, or better. But that's no excuse for giving away what we could use our-
49

selves. It's easy enough for you to be generous, because it's my property you're being generous with. If you had paid for the food, you might think differently about it.'

'In your father's time the order was that the basket should always be well filled. Your father——'

'I know what my father's views were, and I know that he never approved of idiotic squandering . . .'

'Judas! What are you shouting about?'

The noise of their dispute had brought Cyborea into the courtyard, as well as four or five servants who were so happily intent on the quarrel that they were hardly aware of being pushed aside by their angry mistress. 'What's the matter?' she demanded. 'You sound as though you'd caught a thief in the house.'

'I have—or something as bad.'

'I object to that, sir! I was in your father's service for twenty-four years——'

'Be quiet, Barak. And why are you carrying a loaf about?'

'I found it in the beggar's basket. It's full of perfectly good food, and I object to such wicked and nonsensical waste.'

'I suppose the beggars have got to be fed by someone.'

'There's no reason why they should be fed on food that we can eat ourselves!'

'But my dear boy, I've heard you arguing, again and again, that the poor should be properly looked after. And now you object——'

'What I have said, and what I say again, is that there should be a definite social policy in the State. That the poor should be given work, and better wages, and taught to respect themselves. I've never argued in favour of indiscriminate charity, and I strongly object to ruining myself in order to feed a crowd of beggars for whom I'm not responsible, and who won't be a scrap the more grateful.'

'If you'll excuse me, sir, I still resent your suggestion that I'm a thief.'

'I didn't say you were a thief. I said you were a fool.'

'You're making a great fuss about nothing, Judas. What do a few loaves matter? Haven't you anything better to think about than that?'

'Better to think about! Yes, more than any of you! More than you can ever imagine. And now when I'm plagued beyond endurance, worried almost to death, I come home and find there are rats in my barn. Rats eating my substance. Destroying everything. And then you ask if I've got nothing to think about! No, I've got nothing to think about that any of you can understand, or would touch your sympathy if you could.'

'Well, it doesn't do any good to stand there shouting.'

'What do you care——'

'Judas!'

'I won't put out the basket, sir, if that's how you feel about it. Only there'll be a lot of disappointment among the beggars who've always been used to getting a bite at the door.'

'Oh, do what you like.'

'It was always your father's custom, sir.'

'And he showed his wisdom a couple of years ago, didn't he? He died. He'd had enough of living here.'

'That's a brutal thing to say, Judas!'

'Yes, I know. I'm in the wrong again. I'm always in the wrong. I'm in the wrong because I can see

51

forty things that your blind eyes will never guess at !'

He pushed Barak out of the way, and hurrying into the house, shut himself in his room. Presently his anger diminished, and left him in a state of bewildered wretchedness. He had been right—he knew he had been right—in denouncing waste. It was a sinful thing to throw away the crops of the earth and the fruit of men's labour. But somehow or other, so obscurely that he could not remember the way of it, he had been put in the wrong . . . A fuss about nothing, said his mother. Charity and a pious custom, said Barak. But they saw everything so narrowly, from such a meagre height; like wethers grazing, happy with the nearest grass.

There was neither sense nor any hope in the world. There was no hope save in Jesus and his power of bringing to all mankind a light that should illumine their lives with reason and bring forth peace with a sweet smell. He had the power . . . He was, at any rate, the instrument of power. He had said that every-one who acknowledged him would be by him acknow-ledged before God. He was God's agent in the world. Though even as God's agent he was apparently unwill-ing to new-mould society with his own hands, but chose rather to work through the aid of innumerable instruments, which were the hearts and minds of men. He had not given strength enough even to his Disciples. He was the sower of the seed, and he admitted that much of it fell upon stony hearts, and minds that were a tangle of thorns. It was a wasteful system.

But there must be some reason for it . . . Though reason appeared to say that if Jesus wanted to save the souls of all mankind he would do it as quickly and efficiently as possible. For he had the power.

Whether as agent or principal, he had shown over and over again the conquest of mind over matter. He could cure all the diseases of society as simply as everywhere he had cured the loathsome ailments of humble people . . . If it was true, as he had said, that control of all things had been given to him by God. But was that true? For if it was . . .

Faith, faith, he must have faith. Believe in him, and all would be well. Believe in him, in his deep reason for not proving universally his omnipotence. Under Jesus the Omnipotent Benevolence, man would grow less than man, be nothing more than dumb clay in his hands. And thus to belittle man was neither his purpose nor desire.

That was it. That was why so often he held his power in check. As Jesus was necessary to the world of men, so men in their full stature were necessary to him and to his purpose. He was omnipotent, yet he was not self-sufficing. But was such a limitation possible? He had said, Believe in me. But who was he? The Son of Man, the Son of David, the Son of his Father in Heaven. Three in one, and making mystery. Who was he? All he had said was right, was very truth, and yet he himself did not insist on his own infallibility. For he had said that if men spoke against him, they would be forgiven. The unforgivable sin was to speak against the holy Spirit. So he was not one with the holy Spirit, he was not infallible. He might, some day, make a mistake.

He might walk into a trap, and find himself in prison. Or at the foot of the gallows. He might, even now, be asking for advice and wondering most anxiously whether he should take the risk of preaching rebellion in Jerusalem, or flee again to the safety of the hills, the refuge of Galilee. In darkness of the spirit, he might be putting forth his hand to seek a friend who should help him, and finding no one. For in darkness of their own his friends were wrestling with shadows.

Judas threw himself on the bed, face downward to the pillow. His whole body was shaken with his sobbing.

2

In the morning Jesus taught in the Temple. A huge crowd gathered to hear him, but many were disappointed because he did not tell them plainly what they must do, or what he meant to do. He spoke in parables that few could properly understand. They listened with pleasure to his stories of the man who planted a vineyard, and the king who invited all and sundry to the prince's wedding; but they found in these anecdotes nothing that was really helpful except a vague promise of justice. And to some it seemed that justice itself might be rather arbitrary. On the fringes of the multitude there was obvious impatience.

And then a man pushed his way to the front of the crowd, and loudly exclaimed that he wanted to ask a question. He was well-known. He was a money-changer, an irascible fellow who for some time had loudly extolled the Pharisees; many reasons for his adherence to the sect were current, and most of them were scandalous. But nearly everyone was pleased by his intervention, for he was something of a character and he promised to enliven the succession of parables with a little excitement. There was laughter and a mocking cheer when he began to speak, but the noise was quickly hushed.

He began, clumsily, by trying to flatter Jesus. He

did this with the subtlety of an auctioneer, and turned with a wink to draw attention to his cleverness. Then he demanded: 'Tell us what you think about this: is it right to pay taxes to Caesar, or isn't it?'

There was a sudden quiet. A stillness of apprehension fell upon the crowd. This was a question that many had wanted to ask, but most of them were frightened when they heard it. They wanted him to say no, but they knew that *no* meant rebellion, and the nearness of decision made them catch their breath. . . .

'What did he say?'

The muttered question, repeated by a thousand lips, travelled over the crowd like a sudden shower of rain.

'He said, "Show me a coin".'

Jesus took the shilling that the man gave him, and held it out. Those who were nearest him could see what it was. It was a Roman coin, and everyone knew that in the Temple precincts Roman currency was not legal tender. They whispered the news, and it spread through the crowd like a gust of wind in a forest. A Roman coin . . .

'Give Caesar what belongs to Caesar. . . .'

There was a great shout of laughter, and a roar of delight that drowned, for all but those within a yard of him, the rest of the injunction.

Give Caesar what belonged to Caesar, but Caesar had no business in the heart of Judea. What he meant was clear enough, but his cleverness was clear as well-water. They could not take him for sedition on such an answer, though his answer was manifest rebellion. Caesar had no right there . . .

Cushi, the Bethany tanner's friend, was delighted. 'What did I tell you?' he demanded. 'Wasn't I right from the beginning? It's Rome that's the enemy, and always has been. And now he says the same, and we know what to do.'

'God Almighty!' exclaimed the tanner, 'you make me sick. You've got the idea that he's a common ignorant agitator with a one-track mind like your own. Well, he isn't! He's got the only decent brain that's been born in this blasted country for the last five hundred years. All that stuff about the coin was just eye-wash. That money-changer fellow, that stool for the Pharisees, thought he'd got Jesus in a jam, and Jesus showed him the way out. That's all it meant. What you ought to have listened to was the story about the wedding. That parable. What happened there? All the nobs and nobility, all the plutocrats and purse-proud climbers, thought the invitation just meant another of the parties they're always going to, and paid no attention to it. So they got it in the neck. By God, they got it, hot and hard! So then the king sent his servants into the highways and byways, and who did they find there? The poor! Poor bastards like you and me. And they went to the feast. They got pie, and the rich were stinking in their graves.'

'You're right,' said Simon the pedlar. 'That's the story we were meant to listen to. That business about the coin was clever, but it didn't mean anything.'

They were again at the inn where the tanner's cousin was a servant. Amplias called for wine, and said, 'It seemed to me there was a snag in that wedding-story. Why did the poor man get turned out because he hadn't a wedding-garment? He can't expect people like us to buy smart clothes.'

'That was a figure of speech,' said the tanner quickly. 'The man who got kicked out didn't believe in the solidarity of the poor. He wasn't loyal to the interests of his own class.'

'That's a bloody poor explanation,' said Cushi. 'Why the hell should he believe in the solidarity of the poor? I never met anyone except you who. ever thought of such a thing.'

'That's right,' exclaimed Simon the pedlar. 'I've lived all my life among the poor, and you wouldn't ever say I was rich myself, would you? But there isn't any solidarity of feeling between me and the penny-shy, prison-fisted mugs I've got to make a living out of.'

'You've got to educate them,' said the tanner. 'That's what's needed: education.'

'I'm not saying anything against the poor,' Simon explained. 'They're all right in their way. They aren't as clever as the rich, but I daresay they're more honest.'

'I'm getting in a sweat,' said Amplias. 'I'd give anything to know what's going to happen next. Did you see a lot of Temple soldiers in the inner court, and the Roman police in plain clothes? I trod on the foot of one of them, and he hit me in the guts so that I thought I was going to be sick.'

'It's boiling up,' said the tanner. 'It's boiling up for a big show.'

3

Judas stayed all morning in his room, and was torn by the wild beasts of contending thought.

A little after noon Phanuel arrived and asked to see him. Judas sent a message that he had nothing to say. A few minutes later Phanuel came into the room, looking hot and impatient, and immediately began, in a rather ill-tempered fashion, to speak of his own benevolence.

'I'm not going to be put off like this,' he said. 'I came here at great inconvenience to myself, I deliberately took the risk of endangering my reputation with the Sanhedrin—do you realize that? Do you realize it's family affection that induces me to act as mediator, though mediation of any sort is by no means to the liking of many of my colleagues?—and your response is a display of pettiness and ingratitude. But I'm not going to stand it. You can't treat me like this, Judas. I'm your mother's brother, and though you care nothing for me, I care a great deal for you. To stand by, coldly, and see you ruin yourself—I can't do it! Some of my colleagues, naturally enough, don't appreciate my sentiment. They're concerned with the main issue, which is the preservation of the State, and they're quite right in thinking that no personal consideration should stand in their way. But I pleaded with Annas himself. I pleaded for an hour or two's respite, so that I could make one last attempt to persuade you to see reason.'

'I've been looking at reason all morning,' said Judas dully. 'Sometimes it was a whore, smiling, and offering a little pleasure for a price. Sometimes it was a figure with his face hidden, who held out a knife. And sometimes it was a bottomless pit.'

'That's a very fanciful way of putting it.'

'It's three ways.'

'And all of them too fanciful. You're being poetical and obscurantist, and—well, it isn't helpful to talk like that. Not in a time of crisis, such as the present, when we must all be practical.'

'If you want to be practical, why don't you send out your troops and have Jesus arrested now at this very moment? Why do you come to plague and torture me? Why can't you leave me alone?'

'Because, my dear boy, I'm your uncle, and——'

'Because I can be useful to you! Because you're frightened to arrest him in the open, when the crowd is all on his side, and your first move would start the stones flying, and fill the street with rebellion that might trample you and your friends into pulp! That's why you come here, to ask me to put my hand in the coals and save you from burning. But I won't. I can't do it. I can't do anything. Don't you see that I'm not fit to do anything at all?'

'Now come, Judas. This won't do. You must pull yourself together. If you would only believe in me——'

'For God's sake don't say that!'

'But you've got to trust me! For your own sake you must realize that what I propose may be the salvation not only of you, but of the Nazarene, and of countless men and women and children who, by no fault of their own, would suffer the unspeakable horrors of war. Yes, of war! And now I'm being absolutely honest with you. I'm speaking to you as man to man, freely and without reservation. We do fear war. Or at the least, serious rioting. We appreciate the danger of arresting Jesus in public, and though we ourselves do not shrink from that danger, it is our duty to consider the lives of the innocent who would be involved. The women and children. No government worthy of the name can face with equanimity a course of action that would bring suffering to all its people, and death to many. Death to those who are least culpable. And that's why I'm putting my pride in my pocket, and asking you to help us.'

'By betraying him.'

'His conduct in the Temple—this morning he was again inciting the mob to rebellion—has been such as

59

to alienate the sympathy of all right-thinking people. It has become our plain duty to arrest him, and all we have now to decide is the means.'

'So by handing him over to you, I should be putting him in the power of his declared enemies. Yesterday you spoke of protective custody; now you talk of arrest.'

'Now, now. You mustn't twist my words into meaning something I had no intention they should mean. I said his recent conduct had alienated sympathy. I didn't say that he himself had done so. As I told you before, I have a great deal of respect for the man, for his courage, and the novelty of some of his views, and the undoubted cleverness with which he expresses them. But he's dangerous. Much too dangerous. This morning he showed quite clearly that he means to embroil us with Rome, and that, as you know, would be the end of everything. At all costs we must guard against that, and so the simple fact emerges that we can't allow him to remain at liberty any longer.'

'Why not?—I'm sorry, I wasn't thinking. I'm sorry you say that.'

'Yes, we're all sorry. Very sorry indeed that a man with so much ability and such a fine character should set himself against the established order of things. It's a tragedy. I feel it myself, and I know how you must feel it. But we Sadducees have always prided ourselves on our realism. Our ability to face facts. And our task must now be to mitigate that tragedy; to confine it; to keep it from spreading. You see that, don't you?'

'I don't know. I don't think I can. No, don't say anything more! I can't listen to you any longer, or you'll drive me mad with your talk. You're trying to trap me——'

'To help you.'

'I'm beyond help. Look at me! I can't keep my hand still. I couldn't walk without falling, and my brain's worse than that. It's torn to bits, and every word you say is like a hammer nailing another bit of it to the wall. Go and leave me: that's all you can do. Oh yes, I'll think it over. Think it over! As though I hadn't been thinking till every thought's a hundred shreds, and every shred a hundred knots, and every knot in my heart. I'll think it over, but go away, go and leave me now . . .'

4

Towards evening Tamar came in, and sitting on the bed beside Judas began softly to chafe his hands. He made at first a petulant show of resistance, and then submitted. In Tamar's voice and manner there was a new quality of sympathy, a tenderness eager to give and be used. Her ordinary expression of rather sulky indifference was transformed by an awkward but self-conscious enthusiasm. She was like a country girl, warm with dancing and the season of her blood, who with shy determination will give herself to a reluctant lover, or pour on dullard friends the vials of her kindness. She spoke soothingly to Judas, murmured inaptly her unaccustomed endearments.

His appearance distressed her. She got a basin of water, and sponged from his face the cold sweat, and combed the tangle of his hair.

'Poor Judas,' she said. 'Mother told me that Uncle Phanuel had been worrying you again. But you mustn't mind what he says. He just doesn't understand.'

Phanuel, she said, was an old man who had lost the knack of seeing things in their proper aspect. To him the world was occupied only by people who travelled in his own way of life, by events that kept it smooth, that prolonged it; and on the other side, by men and circumstances that impeded or threatened his way. He could not understand a new thing, nor perceive any greater sort of truth than the little truths which served his own advantage. He was like a farmer, cunning in the management of his cattle and his crops, but ignorant of all that lived outside his few acres. She grew more passionate in her denunciation : Phanuel was a stupid man, she said, and not worth listening to.

'You're wrong,' said Judas. 'He's clever. Cleverer than you or I.'

'But not wise! We know things—you and I—that he's never guessed at. I used to like him, and admire him, and think he was a better man than father, because he was always so sure of himself, and successful in everything he did. But I was wrong. Father was often unhappy and bad-tempered, but that was because he had a far bigger ambition than Uncle Phanuel. He wanted to understand things, and he was unhappy because he was always being disappointed. I see it quite clearly now. Oh, I wish he was still alive, so that I could tell him! And if he was alive he'd be on your side, Judas. I'm sure of that. So don't bother about what Uncle Phanuel says. He wants you to promise to have nothing more to do with Jesus, I suppose——'

'He wants more than that. He wants me to help the Sanhedrin to arrest him. It's got to be done quietly, to avoid trouble with the crowd.'

'But that's unthinkable! It's foul and beastly! I

never thought it was anything so bad as that. Oh, poor Judas!'

'That's what he came about yesterday afternoon, but I told him I couldn't do it.'

'Of course you couldn't! And you've warned Jesus, haven't you? You've told him about the danger of his being arrested?'

'No. Not yet.'

'But you must! You can't let him go about without knowing what they're planning. That's almost as bad as actually betraying him. Judas, you must go and tell him at once!'

'That's your opinion, is it?'

'Of course it is. You've no choice——'

'No, I've noticed that. I've no choice because everybody else chooses for me. Mother, and Uncle Phanuel, and you. You all know exactly what I should do. I'm the ox in the mill, and I've got to grind your corn. But you all want it ground in your own way, so one of you pulls me against the sun, another pricks me into it. To hell with the ox. He doesn't matter. He's only a fool who doesn't know what's good for him.'

'Oh, darling, what do you mean? You're talking nonsense, aren't you? There's no question about it: Jesus is right, and Uncle Phanuel wrong, and——'

'I don't agree.'

'That Jesus is right?'

'That Uncle Phanuel is wrong. Listen to me. You've got to get this into your head: there may be civil war at any moment—there's certain to be rioting—and that means that countless men and women and helpless children will be maimed and destroyed. Death's round the corner. Death for those who are least culpable, suffering for every living soul. Jesus is challenging not only the Sanhedrin, but Rome. Rome! Uncle

Phanuel says there's no doubt about it. And war with Rome would mean annihilation. Even if we escaped with our lives, there'd be nothing left to make life tolerable. This house and all we possess would be taken from us, and our only neighbours would be misery and wounds and widows howling. Have you ever considered—have you ever pictured for one minute—the horrors of war?'

'Yes, of course I have. I suppose everybody has, at one time or another. I'm quite sure that Jesus has.'

'And what has that got to do with it?'

'Don't be so silly, Judas. It means that he'll do all he can to avoid war, because he loves people and doesn't want to cause them unnecessary suffering. But if war is needed, then it must be his will, and so we can't grumble and we haven't got to worry. Because his will is all that matters, and we can trust him absolutely.'

'How long have you believed that?'

'Oh, not long. It doesn't take long to see the truth when it's made so clear. I've been listening to him, this morning and yesterday, and talking to some of the women who follow him.'

'And now you're a believer too?'

'Of course I am.'

'Of course!'

'It's impossible not to be. Oh darling, if only I'd taken your advice months ago, when you told me I should go to him! It would have meant half-a-year in heaven.'

Judas looked at her sourly.

'It's absolutely true,' she said earnestly. 'I've never been so happy before. I never knew what happiness meant till now.'

'Yes, I felt like that at one time. But wait a bit,

and you'll see the other side of the medal. Wait a bit and he'll make you so damnably miserable that you'll wish you had never been born.'

'That only happens when people begin to doubt him.'

'What the hell do you know about it? About him, or doubt, or anything at all? You've been one of his beglamoured fools for forty-eight hours, and I've been one for nearly three years! You can't tell me anything about him. You can't even tell me this, you can't answer the simple question : If Jesus so loves the world, why does he want to turn it upside down and ruin the livelihood of thousands of people for the very dubious benefit of paupers, prostitutes, and Jewish Nationalists?'

'He doesn't, and you know he doesn't.'

'I don't care. I'm past caring. But I think, I think I know, that Phanuel's right. No one is justified in creating anarchy to achieve his own ends, whatever they are. We want peace and happiness, and that's all that's worth bothering about. If God didn't mean men to be happy, then he'd no right to create man. And when we've succeeded in being happy in spite of him he's got no right to take our happiness from us. He's got no right to say the poor are worth more than the rich. They're not! They're foul and dirty, and Jesus is ashamed of them, and that's why he's going to rob the rich, to cover their scabs and scars and filthy nakedness with our coats. He's going to upset the whole world, because God's made a stinking mess of it, and they hate the sight of it, and no wonder. *We* have done better than God : we've created peace and order and beauty in our own lives. We've made living a gracious and lovely thing, and now like a thief in the night he's coming to steal our property. But I

65

C

won't have it, I won't let him! I'm going to do what Phanuel wants me to do, and that's to save civilization. I'll go and see Jesus, and find out where he's going. I'll see him once more, I'll see him once more . . .'

His voice, that had risen to a dry scream, now dwindled to a hoarse and shaken whisper. The muscles of his face contracted, and showed through the skin like the tendons of an old man's hand. Tearless but red-rimmed, his eyes grew bloodshot, and in the violent agitation that seized his body his teeth began to chatter as loudly as old bones rattling together.

Tamar crouched sobbing at his feet. Her body, relaxed, was shapeless and heavy, her plump back was tremulous. Weeping, she cried again and again, 'You don't mean it, Judas, you don't mean it.'

He made no answer, and presently looking up she was frightened by the mortal set of his features. With a quick ungainly movement she lifted herself on to the bed beside him, and flinging her arms rounds his shoulders, held him tightly in a clumsy embrace. She rocked him to-and-fro, as though trying to warm and waken him out of his nearness to death.

He struggled weakly, disliking the close heat of her body and the strong perfume she used. But she held him still, and he submitted to the growing sensation of comfort. He let his weight fall wholly on her, and laying him down she stretched herself beside him, still caressing him, and telling him he was mistaken, he was not himself, and that by-and-by he would feel better.

5

Phanuel had been waiting for a couple of hours in the High Priest's palace. Caiaphas was there, and had heard the failure of his mission without exhibiting much surprise or making any new suggestion. He was an extremely handsome man of about fifty, with big heavy-lidded eyes, spaced far apart, a resolutely curving nose, a finely shaped mouth, a short brown beard; and an air of effectual probity. His appearance did all that was possible to mask his incompetence, and his usual expression was unshaken dignity.

They were waiting for Annas, who was with the Procurator, and to Phanuel the delay was tedious. But Caiaphas made amiable conversation, and remained perfectly calm.

'Here he is now,' said Phanuel at last, and through the doorway came a short, broad-shouldered, heavily-built old man, who as he entered glared at each in turn, and growled: 'He won't do it. He says it's our job, and he won't touch it.'

Annas was a remarkable figure. His swarthy face was large, and seemed larger than it was by reason of the dense beard that grew outward from his cheek-bones, covered his jowl with its thick grey fleece, and from his chin jutted and descended in a white-and-tawny fall. He was deeply wrinkled, and his coarse skin, corrugated and discoloured, seemed to lie loosely on his forehead, his fleshy nose, and sagging cheeks. His eyes were small, bright brown in a yellow-flecked circumference, and their ill-temper was exaggerated by overhanging brows and the heavy bull-like movement of his head.

He sat down, ponderously, and growled again: 'He says it's a religious dispute, and he doesn't feel qualified to deal with dogma and exegesis, confound him.'

'You mean the Procurator?' asked Caiaphas.

Annas ignored him. 'I used every argument I could,

but nothing'll move him. He won't order the arrest. He won't raise a finger to help us. And I wouldn't either if I was in his place. It's the chance of a lifetime for him.'

'He's an ambitious man,' said Phanuel gloomily.

'And makes no attempt to hide it.'

'He advertises it,' said Phanuel. 'Will you ever forget his arrival, when he came in with colours flying, and his regiments set up their ensigns as if they'd captured the whole country? And yet he's very pleasant to meet—he has always been perfectly charming to me—and I can't help being disappointed in him. It's unpleasant to see a man so ruthlessly intent on his own interests.'

Caiaphas began : 'If only he would realize that, in this matter at least, our interests are identical——'

'They aren't,' said Annas.

Caiaphas was mildly puzzled : 'I don't see how they can be anything else. Surely it's to the advantage of the Imperial government, as well as to us, that sedition should be quelled as soon as possible?'

'It isn't to Pilate's advantage !' exclaimed Annas. 'He can only fish in troubled waters, and if Jesus of Nazareth wages war against the High Priest of Jerusalem, he'll be delighted. Because civil war brings him in as mediator, and he stays on as master. That's his game, and it's a good one too. Only it doesn't happen to suit us.'

'I'm afraid you're right,' said Phanuel.

'But that's only guess-work,' Caiaphas protested. 'You've no proof that what you say is correct, and I don't believe it is. In my opinion that Procurator's a thoroughly honest man—perhaps rather limited, as so many Romans are—and it seems to me that he shows a very proper sense of his position by refusing to interfere in a matter that pertains only to the Church.'

'A matter that pertains only to the Church wouldn't have brought me back to the Council,' said Annas brutally. And turning to Phanuel asked: 'How did you get on with Judas?'

'Inconclusively. It would be wrong to say that I have made no impression on him, but it would be misleading to pretend that he is ready to fall in with our wishes.'

'You've failed, in fact? You've been butting your head against a brick wall, just as I've been doing with Pilate?'

'No, I won't admit that. My project was far from hopeless. Nothing like yours, nothing like it at all. Frankly, my dear Annas, I'd have been surprised if the Procurator had accepted the responsibility of arresting Jesus. Very much surprised. I thought you might have persuaded him to give us a little help in one way or another, but that was the limit of my expectation. From what I heard of him, when I was in Rome a few months ago——'

'At the moment, Phanuel, I'm not interested in Roman gossip. I'm interested only in Jerusalem, and only in one problem in Jerusalem: how are we going to get the Nazarene arrested without setting the whole town ablaze? Pilate could do it, but for reasons of his own he won't. Your romantic nephew Judas could help us, but he won't either; and I suppose he's got reasons of some kind for his refusal. So both those ways are closed to us, and we've got to look for something else. What is it going to be?'

'Perhaps,' said Caiaphas, 'we might persuade Phanuel to continue his good offices with Judas. A clever and headstrong young man cannot be weaned overnight from his loyalties, however absurd they are. It takes time. It may take a long time——'

'And long before then there'll be internecine war in Judea, Rome will be called in to suppress it, the Sanhedrin will be abolished as the price of peace, and a couple of regiments of Roman infantry will be drilling in the Temple. My good Caiaphas, we've not only got to solve the problem, but we've got to solve it before the end of the week.'

'I believe,' said Phanuel, 'that the Nazarene's followers are by no means united.' He spoke coldly, for Annas had offended him by interrupting his disquisition on the character of Pilate.

'They're no more united than a fistful of sand,' said Annas.

'In Rome,' said Phanuel, 'there's a well-known aphorism: *Divide et impera*.'

'Good,' said Annas. 'And how do you propose to do it?'

'It shouldn't be difficult to persuade the people of Jerusalem that they have no common cause with Galilean Zealots.'

'I had thought of that,' said Annas. 'We can do that. And I've got an idea,' he continued, 'that it might be useful to spread the rumour that Jesus is being paid by Rome.'

'Paid to create trouble?'

Annas nodded.

Caiaphas, very astonished, exclaimed: 'But surely there's no truth in that? It's the first I've heard of it, and I must say that I find it very difficult to believe.'

'I don't care whether you believe it or not. It's the people in the street I'm thinking of.'

'We can make capital,' said Phanuel, 'out of some of his more obvious heresies.'

70

'I was going to leave that to the Pharisees. They'll enjoy it, and do it better than we should.'

'And the instruments?'

'Agents, you mean? Well, there's the department we always rely on for under-cover work, and the police have given me the names of about a hundred people who can be trusted, they say, to stir up plenty of trouble if they're properly paid.'

'Let them be paid most generously,' said Caiaphas. 'An occasion like this is no time to think of economy.'

'They'll be paid all right. In fact I've paid some of them already. You've no objection?'

'Of course not. We're in your hands entirely, Annas.'

'Then that's all right. Now as to Jesus himself: so far I've found it quite impossible to get accurate information about his plans—I was relying chiefly on Judas, of course. But I've made arrangements for him to be more closely watched in future, and if he goes wandering about by himself, we'll take a chance and arrest him right away. Otherwise I'm not going to provoke trouble. We'll do all we can to divide the crowd, but with that exception, for a couple of days at least, we remain inactive. The troops will be standing-by in case of emergency, but I think we ought to be uncommonly slow to recognize an emergency till it's ripe to bursting-point.'

'That sounds risky,' said Phanuel, 'but I think on the whole it's wise.'

'I'm sure it is.'

There was a short silence, and then Caiaphas, rising with easy dignity, remarked: 'Well, if everything has been decided I think I shall leave you. It has been a tiring day, hasn't it? But if you want me again, you know where to find me, of course. Good-bye, Phanuel.

71

You're being a great help to us. I shall see you to-morrow, Annas.'

'A fool of a man,' said Annas, when Caiaphas had gone.

'I often find an oddness in the thought that he is your son-in-law,' said Phanuel.

'It was a good match for Sarah.'

'Oh, very good.'

'She's fond of him, too . . . There's one other thing, Phanuel. I think Judas ought to be watched. He must have got a very good idea, in a general way, of what we've been saying and thinking——'

'I assure you I've been discretion itself. I told him nothing except our decision that Jesus was to be arrested at the earliest opportunity. For his own good, I said. I used the phrase, protective custody, I think.'

'Well, if he warns Jesus——'

'He won't. I'm sure he can be trusted not to do that. It would be an abuse of confidence.'

'I've known such a thing to happen, Phanuel. And as a measure of security I propose to tell the police to have Judas followed. It won't do him any harm, and it may be useful to us to know when and where he meets Jesus. You don't really object, do you?'

'No, I suppose not. Not if you think it advisable. Though it isn't pleasant to think of one's nephew being shadowed.'

'Well, that's all we can do for the present . . . I'm getting old, Phanuel. Too old for this kind of thing. But I hate to think of Pilate sitting there laughing at us, and I hate still more to think of him marching his eagles into the Temple. And he won't, if I can help it. I'll be damned if he does, though I break a thousand Nazarenes to stop him!'

WEDNESDAY

1

JUDAS and Tamar were walking to Bethany. Late the night before they had started to go there, but turned back because the road was said to be unsafe. Several people had been robbed and beaten by hooligans who were taking advantage of the general disturbance, and others had been frightened by troops of young Galileans whose patriotism sought release in rowdy mischief. Two men and a woman, sober middle-aged people, had warned Judas and his sister against travelling by night. They themselves had just escaped from a band of northern Zealots, and one of the men had a bruise on his cheek, the woman's dress was torn . . . But now, beneath a blue-and-cloudy sky, the day-lit road was comforting, and the many people on their way to Bethany made a friendly noise.

To Judas, however, the road was unreal, like a road in a foreign land; as he seemed himself, or part of him, to have become a stranger and not wholly real. There was a fragment of his consciousness that sat on his shoulder and watched him with a nearly impersonal interest. So you have made up your mind and you are going to warn him, said the piece on his shoulder. Well, action of some kind is almost inevitable, and action is always interesting. And the physical part of him—the legs moving, the chest filling, eyes and nostrils aware of occupation—found in easy progress a certain timid enjoyment. But in the core of his being, that felt his body and listened to the watcher on his shoulder, was a dull fever. As if in that complexity of dreaming, when a man, caught between certain memory and apparent chimera, will struggle against unconsciousness to see whether he is sleeping or awake, his inner self was feebly wrestling to find some explanation of what seemingly had happened, to focus thought on that which surely threatened. It was out of a mingled nightmare of reality and dreadful fancy that Tamar had rescued him, but the manner of the rescue—the dispelling of fear, the evoking of a partial strength—was now half-forgotten in the procession of phantoms, more immediate than reality, that had filled his later sleep. He had cried to her, again and again, 'Then you mustn't leave me!' and she as often, or more often, had told him she would stay with him as long as he wanted her: so much he knew was real. And she was still beside him, and that was comforting. The deepest part of him was aware of a continuing apprehension, but his body that contained him, and his legs that carried him forward, knew a perverse and minor satisfaction. And the watcher on his shoulder, as a heartless spectator will, was mildly enjoying himself.

To Tamar, making some idle remark, Judas heard himself replying in a dry and distant voice; but sensibly enough. The hill-side, grey-green with olives, was behind them, and a rank of trees threw its tangled shadow on the road and the people before. A few yards in front of them was a group of men, confident in their demeanour and loud-talking. Some of them were tall beyond the average, and broadly built. Tamar was making guesses at their style of life and the country they came from, and Judas, answering again, grew more accustomed to his voice. The sound of it restored him a little, as though by speech he was re-integrating himself.

'Those two big ones come from the north,' she said.

'I don't think so. I've seen one of them before—he was with us when we came—and he didn't speak like a Galilean. He's a tanner, I think. And the smaller one, the fat one, was there too.'

'And the very broad man, who walks like a soldier, what do you think he is?'

'I don't know. Perhaps he has been a soldier.'

'Talking about the fellow in the blue coat?' asked someone at Judas's elbow. 'Yes, he's been a soldier, though he wouldn't admit it, if you asked him.'

It was a quiet-seeming, respectable-looking man who had spoken. He appeared friendly, disposed for conversation, and fell into step with Judas. He had a companion, rather older, a little wheezy and very red in the nose, who also aligned himself with them, and walked beside Tamar. He too was affable, and remarked on the pleasant morning. They were artisans, by the look of them, and the man who spoke first had a frank and pleasant face, though his near profile was made a little ungainly by an injury to his left ear. The top and part of the wing had been cut off.

'Why doesn't he like to admit that he has been a soldier? The big man, I mean?' asked Tamar.

'He's a deserter,' said Crop-ear. 'From Roman service.'

'A very bad character,' said Red Nose.

'A criminal record,' explained Crop-ear.

'I think he looks a nice man,' said Tamar.

'Oh, he's got lots of friends,' said Red Nose.

'His name's Barabbas,' added Crop-ear. 'He's well-known.'

There was a little silence, and Red Nose made another comment on the fine weather they were having.

'Going to Bethany?' asked Crop-ear.

'Yes.'

'So are we.'

'It looks like everybody had the same idea,' said Red Nose genially. 'I was just saying, just before we met you, what a fine thing it is to be living at a time like this. It's inspiring, isn't it?'

'He's a wonderful man, the Nazarene,' said Crop-ear.

'You mean the Christ,' said Red Nose with a cough.

Judas whispered to Tamar: 'Can't we get rid of them?'

'I don't like to insult them,' she answered. 'They're terribly silly, but so friendly.'

'You know him, I suppose?' asked Crop-ear.

'I do.'

'What's he going to do next? It's about time he made a definite move, isn't it?'

Judas made no reply.

'Mum's the word, eh?' said Crop-ear, unabashed. 'Well, I'm not asking you to tell any secrets. It's just friendly interest on my part. Everybody's interested in what's going to happen next.'

'Of course they are,' said Red Nose. 'Especially people like us, that think so highly of him. Is he going to preach to-day?'

'Sure to be,' said Crop-ear. 'But where? At Bethany or in the Temple?'

Judas, his voice breaking, shouted: 'I don't know,

and I don't want to discuss it. I don't want to talk to you.'

'All right, all right! No need to lose your temper, is there?'

'We were only asking for a bit of innocent information,' protested Red Nose.

'Well, go away! I want nothing to do with you, and I won't be pestered by you!'

A few yards in front of them, the tanner and his friends were attracted by the loud distress of Judas's voice, and turned to see what was the matter. The tanner recognized him.

'Anything wrong, sir?'

'Tell these men to go away.'

'Worrying you, are they?—Well, get to hell out of here! This gentleman's a friend of mine, and you're not. So push off!'

Red Nose and Crop-ear made indignant protestation, and a small crowd began to collect. The bare black head of Barabbas was taller than the men about him, and above the chattering sounded a screeching gasp of pain as he hit Crop-ear in the belly.

Judas, trembling, seized Tamar by the arm. The little fat man, who was Amplias, came to them and said, 'You go on, you don't want to be mixed up in all this. Everybody's excited to-day, and there may be a bit of a row. No, don't worry about my friends. They're all right. They can look after themselves. Go on, it's quite all right, and you can't do any good standing here.'

For a little distance they had the road to themselves, and Judas said, 'I didn't mean to create a scene, but I couldn't help it. I couldn't stand those fellows. Their vulgar loathsome triviality. But my nerves are all on edge.'

'I know, dear. They were rather awful, though they didn't mean to be. But you're all right now, aren't you?'

'Yes, I'm all right.'

'Wasn't the man they called Barabbas magnificent? I don't believe he's really bad. He doesn't look bad.'

'I didn't notice.'

2

The village of Bethany was full of people. They nearly hid it from sight, as if a cloud of locusts—black and many-coloured—had settled upon it. They stood patiently, crowding the lanes, and made talkative groups in doorways, and alleys cool in shadow. Tamar made inquiry, and found that Jesus and some of the Twelve were in the house of a man called Simon, who had been a leper till Jesus cured him.

In the narrow street that led to it the people stood shoulder to shoulder, breast to back; and they had to force their way through the thickness of the crowd. Bartholomew, one of the Twelve, stood at the door and let them in. He was a burly good-humoured man, and there were beads of sweat like raindrops on his forehead. He had a fine resonant voice, and he greeted Judas loudly.

'Well, where have you been for the last couple of days? We all thought you'd deserted.' And to Tamar he said with laugh, 'They wouldn't miss me if they didn't see me for a month, but we can't get on without him. He carries the purse.'

'He hasn't been well,' said Tamar.

In a large outer room there were a dozen people or more; men and women. Of the Disciples, Philip and

78

Thomas and Matthew, once a tax-collector, were there. They were talking together, and all of them, unlike Bartholomew, were looking worried and out of humour. Matthew, a pale and haggard man with bright black-circled eyes, made a gesture of relief when he saw Judas, and came quickly towards him. He asked the same question as Bartholomew, but his voice was irritable, his manner impatient.

'He has been ill,' said Tamar quickly. 'I am his sister, and I've been looking after him.'

'Fever?' he asked.

'No, he was just worn-out. But he's better now.'

'We were getting rather anxious,' said Matthew.

'I suppose you've heard what happened yesterday?' asked Thomas gloomily.

'No, what was it? I've heard nothing. Has anything happened to him?'

'You can talk about that later,' Matthew interrupted. 'I'd better go and tell Peter you're here. He's got to make preparation for to-morrow, and he wants some money. You've got some, I hope?'

'A little,' said Judas.

'He won't need very much. We're having supper together, he and the twelve of us. I'll tell Peter you've come.'

He went into the next room.

'What has happened?' asked Judas again.

Thomas hesitated, looked at Tamar, and said, 'Well, perhaps it wasn't as serious as we thought. It was only a few of us who were really upset.'

'I'll go and talk to those women,' said Tamar. 'I shan't leave you,' she whispered to Judas.

Thomas and Philip watched her as she went towards a group that consisted of two women, a thin excited girl, a restless small boy, and a very old man with a long but scanty beard. The women were hip-spread voluble mothers, thickset and of resolute appearance.

'I don't like speaking of it, except among ourselves,' said Thomas, 'but the fact is he made a bad mistake yesterday.'

'He made a speech that created a very unfortunate impression,' explained Philip.

'We'd left Jerusalem,' Thomas continued, 'and gone up the hill. There was a crowd following, as usual, and suddenly he got angry and let loose a spate of prophecy and denunciation that made most of them shake in their shoes. It frightened me, and I'm used to him. He was like a Roman general—one of the good ones—and Jeremiah and the Angel of Wrath all rolled into one. I've never heard anything like it. It was magnificent, if you like, but he should never have let himself say what he did.'

'It was a tactical blunder of gigantic proportion,' said Philip.

'What did he say?'

'Well, it's difficult to remember exactly, but he certainly foretold the destruction of the Temple, and a period of world-wide panic, misery, and war. A punishment for sin, of course. He said the Jews would have to live under the heel of the Gentiles as long as there were any Gentiles left.'

'That was going too far,' said Philip. 'It was a pity he said that.'

'He said that heaven and earth would pass away, but his words would live for ever.'

'At that point there was a good deal of interruption,' said Philip.

'But what made him so angry?' asked Judas.

'The usual thing. He saw a poor woman and felt
80

sorry for her. That was while we were still in the Temple. There were a lot of well-to-do people giving very handsomely to the priest at the door—you can't say that the rich in Jerusalem aren't generous—and then he saw this woman, obviously as poor as an out-of-work cobbler's widow, and as old as the hills, come hobbling up to drop a couple of farthings in the plate. Well, that did for him. He went up in a flame—you know the way he does—and told everybody that she'd put in more than all the rest of them heaped-up together. You could see him burning as he said it.'

'He is the only man I have ever known,' said Philip, 'in whom compassion has the vehemence of wrath.'

'He was still smouldering when we climbed the hill, and then, without any reason so far as I could see, the flames shot up again. I'll never forget it. He promised that those who remained faithful to him would survive, but that was forgotten in the general effect, which was terrifying. Nation rising against nation, woe to women who give suck, the ruin of Jerusalem, fathers betraying sons, and persecution all round : that's part of what he said, and that's the part that most of the crowd will remember. I know I shall. I felt my heart shrivelling.'

'You see the magnitude of his error,' said Philip solemnly. 'To take the heart out of people whom you wish to support you is not the way to success.'

'Some of them may have been his enemies,' said Judas. 'It's a good thing to take the heart out of your enemies. The road here, and Bethany itself, are crowded with people who certainly don't bear him ill-will for anything he has said.'

'These are mostly country people,' said Philip. 'But I have reason to believe that his prophecy of the

81

destruction of Jerusalem is keenly resented in the city itself.'

'Here's Peter now,' said Thomas.

Heavy-footed, his broad body in a cloak that fluttered and flapped with the energy of his movements, Peter hurried towards them, and flinging his great arms round Judas kissed him on both cheeks.

'My boy, my boy!' he exclaimed. 'Where have you been? You haven't been well? You're not looking well. Never mind, you'll soon be better. Have you got any money with you? That's good, that's fine. Well, come into the other room and have a talk. There's a tremendous crowd, I'm afraid, but he's there and he'll be delighted to see you.'

'I wonder what has been wrong with him?' said Thomas, as Judas went with Peter into the inner room. 'He's looking like death.'

'He is nervous and high-strung,' said Philip, 'but like all nervous people he has great power of recuperation.'

'I wish I had more,' said Matthew, and turned suddenly to listen.

From the street outside came a various noise of exclamation, jeering, and good humour. The outer door was thrown open, and a woman appeared, her rose-red silk-mantled back to the room as she shouted to the people in the street: 'Never you mind where I got them! But I didn't get them for nothing, no more than you got that black eye for nothing . . . Well, that's better than looking as if you'd spent all your life scratching yourself on an ash-heap. It's a poor heart that never rejoices, so put that in your porridge and choke on it!'

She turned, and the door shut behind her. She was dressed in great splendour, and with many jewels, and though no longer young her beauty at first sight was startling. She primmed her yellow dress, and shook her mantle to a handsomer fold, and laughed.

'There's no use buying pretty clothes to keep them in a box under your bed, is there?' she demanded. There was a ring of defiance in her voice, but a ring that trembled slightly and threatened to break. She moved from the door, and the light falling on her revealed a decade of years that the shadows had hidden. Her face was heavier than it had been in youth, her eyes more deeply set. But in the late summer of her loveliness there was still a glow that took the colour from the gold and rubies of her abundant jewellery. The women in the room looked at her with stony gaze and lips grown thin, but Philip and Thomas greeted her with uneasy friendship. She had been very generous to them in the past.

Thomas said to her, 'I'm not sure if you can see him, Mary, but I'll go and find out.'

'The inner room,' said Philip confidingly, as Thomas left them, 'is hardly so commodious as one might wish. Otherwise, of course——'

Mary pleaded with him: 'Let me in just for a minute or two! I've got something for him.'

'You may leave it with me, if you like.'

'No, that's no good, that wouldn't be the same thing at all. My God, Philip, I wish you looked less like a graven image and more like a human being!'

An elderly man, prim-featured and self-satisfied, turned and said solemnly, 'That is no way to speak to one of the Twelve!' But Philip answered calmly, 'Do I look like an image? I must confess that I have never paid much attention to my appearance.'

'Well, you ought to,' said Mary, 'for other people's sake, if not for your own.'

From the women in the room, most of whom were elderly and unhandsome, there came the hiss and gabble of angry comment, and a voice said clearly: 'A dress like that is simply indecent.'

'Indecent, is it!' Mary, hot with a sudden temper, turned on the speaker. 'It's a damned sight less indecent than that dingy remnant of respectability that you put on in the dark this morning. If you want to know my opinion of indecency, it's coming to see *him* with a look on your face and a rag on your back that are only fit for sitting up with a corpse. Is that clear? Well, get this clear too: I'm about tired of hearing funny remarks about my clothes, and I don't want any more of them, from you or anyone else!'

One of the solidly severe women, with whom Tamar had been talking, took a step forward, clenching her fists, and in a voice that trembled with a strange fury, said: 'Do you consider it proper to come here dressed like a harlot?'

'Yes! And I'll tell you why!'

Philip put a restraining hand on Mary's shoulder, but she pushed him away. 'It's all right,' she said. 'I'm not going to lose my temper. There's nothing to lose it about. She doesn't know who I am, that's all. But I'm going to tell her.'

She faced the thickset woman and spoke in a hard but even voice that rose gradually to a scornful triumph: 'I'm Mary of Magdala, and I am a harlot —or I was till a year ago, and having seen a bit of respectable society since I gave it up, I'm not ashamed of my trade. I've met a lot of people like you, and that woman there, in the last few months. People who dress like you, and think like you, and what they think is as shabby as their clothes. And you've all got

84

the same disease, and that's fear. Yes, fear! You're afraid now. You're afraid of me! You think I'm going to create a scene and make you ashamed of being in the same room with me. You're afraid of *him*, in case he does anything outrageous that'll strip you mother-naked——'

'Mary, be quiet! You have no right to make such an accusation.' Philip, his gravity become indignant, seemed to grow in stature, and he rebuked her with a dignity that would have silenced a lesser woman. But Mary was still rebellious.

'There is no one here,' he said, 'who is not his assured and loving friend. And to impugn their fidelity is to offer insult to him.'

'Oh no, it isn't! He's got to take his friends as he finds them, and he knows that as well as I do. He's not easily taken in by a smug face and a bit of Sunday piety, no more than I am.'

'You put yourself on his level, do you?' asked a tall thin man with heavy eyebrows and trembling hands.

'No, I don't do that. But he and I have got the same sort of outlook in some ways. We're not impressed by a lot of things that seem so important to you that you can't ever see over the top of them. We're not respectable, in your meaning of the word, and we don't give a damn for what other people think.'

The room was not so large than anyone could wholly ignore her. There were some who tried, but her rich voice assailed their isolation, her charges stabbed them in the back. They turned frowning faces and glared across their shoulders. Their neighbours, with less discipline or more conscience, noisily disputed, and the two thickset women were demanding that she be thrown out. Tamar stood by herself, held as in a vice between horror and fascination. The tainted luxury of Mary's beauty had captured her imagination, and she felt like searching fingers the hard points of truth in her intemperate criticism.

Half-pleading for quietness, half-commanding it, Philip spoke again, and the clamour lessened. He tried to draw Mary farther away from the inner door, but she resisted him.

'What has made you so angry?' he asked. 'This isn't your usual temper.'

'Ask him, and her,' she said, and pointed to the woman who had said her dress was indecent, to the thin man with the trembling hands. 'They were at the meeting last night, and heard the treachery that was spoken. And now, like the crawling canting respectable traitors they are, they've come here to fawn and slobber on him, and tell him they're his true devoted friends. Isn't that enough to make an honest woman angry?'

'Be quiet!' said Philip again, as the hubbub broke anew. 'What meeting was this?'

'After he'd been speaking on the hill,' said Mary. 'After he warned them about the destruction of the Temple and the war that's coming. That was too much for them. They began to think their own skins were in danger, so they got together and chattered like old women and passed a resolution saying they thought he had gone too far. Gone too far! That's always their cry if anyone steps outside their own dingy little street, or thinks of anything new. They're getting ready to rat: that's what they meant!'

'Is this true?' asked Philip.

'It's a very garbled account of a discussion we had,' said the man.

86

'There's not a word of truth in it!' exclaimed the woman beside him. 'She's lying. A woman like that is always a liar.'

'I've spoken nothing but the truth,' said Mary, 'and you'll discover it soon enough. They're beginning to rat. They don't like danger, they're frightened for their skins. They know he's right, they know he's mercy and truth and justice, he's the only thing in life that makes life worth living. But that doesn't matter to them, they won't think of that, because he's dangerous! It's their skins they're worrying about, and the houses they've built, and the money they've swindled out of their neighbours' pockets. They're getting ready to run, they're going to save their necks and their property and let him look after himself. That's what they're going to do, and that's why I've come to see him, to tell him there's a few that'll stand with him no matter what happens. I'm not afraid! You never heard of a whore running away, did you? Not from all the world. We know the world, and we don't give a damn for it. It's nothing but lust and lies and rottenness. But he's mercy, I tell you, he's beauty and truth and justice, and all I am and everything I have is his to do as he likes with, now and for evermore!'

The inner door was opened, and Thomas called softly to her: 'Mary!'

3

The door closed behind her, and those who remained in the outer room looked at each other in some discomfort. They made tentative observations and consolatory remarks.

'Of course, women of that sort are often very emotional.'

'I dare say she feels quite deeply, but still . . .'

'She should never have been allowed to come here.'

'One must, at all costs, preserve a certain balance . . .'

'. . . and say what you like, her dress was *not* suitable.'

'One must think clearly.'

'. . . and take a realistic view of the situation.'

'It is easy for her, because she has no responsibilities.'

'The trouble with idealists is that they are not practical.'

'. . . and one has got to face facts.'

From the inner room came the sound of many voices in exclamation. It was like the noise of people startled by a daring acrobat, or shocked by a sentence of doom. Then came a single voice, high-pitched, protesting . . . and Tamar made a frightened movement to the door. But silence followed, or someone speaking so gently that nothing could be heard in the outer room. But they listened still, with expressions of anxiety.

The door between was thrown open, and Judas, white of face and clumsy-footed, came in. He looked round him, and saw Tamar, and took her by both hands.

'I didn't mean to speak,' he said, 'but I couldn't help myself. It was so monstrous, so imbecile and wicked a thing to do. And he defended her.'

'What happened?' said Tamar. 'We heard a noise . . .'

'Tell us what she did!'

'What did she say?'

'Mary is an honest creature, but unpredictable and violent,' said Philip.

'She came in,' said Judas, his voice quick and high, 'she came in and told him that she loved him better than life. She made a lot of wild statements. It was very embarrassing, but he smiled and said "Let her be." Then she took out a jar of perfume—she was crouching at his feet—it was an alabaster jar and the most expensive sort of nard. It must have been worth ten or twelve pounds. And she anointed his forehead and his feet. She spilled ten pounds' worth of perfume on him, and he put his hand on her head and smiled.'

'I suppose money means nothing to her.'

'Easy come, easy go.'

'If I had ten pounds to spare,' said the thin man, 'I think I could spend it more usefully than that.'

'Or give it to the poor. Heaven knows there's plenty of poverty in the world,' spoke the virtuous voice of one of the thickset women.

'That's what I said,' cried Judas. 'It was so utterly senseless a thing to do. It was just throwing money away.'

'A piece of vulgar ostentation,' said one of the women.

'Yes,' said Judas, 'but he didn't think so. I told her she ought to be ashamed of herself. I told her that money wasn't meant to be wasted, and he said "Let her alone." I said she ought to have sold the perfume and given the money to the poor. And he said, "The poor are with you always, but you will not always have me." '

'That's not the point,' said the thin man.

'There was no sense in it!' exclaimed Judas. He still held Tamar by the wrist, but now he flung her from him and spoke with increasing violence. 'He's not normal, is he? Things have been too much for him, don't you think? And he doesn't know what he's doing. We've got to think for ourselves now. If he was normal he wouldn't let himself be anointed by a whore. He wouldn't, would he?'

4

On a shelf of rock, a little distance from the road and above it, Judas sat and tried to straighten in his memory its tangle of words and emotion, of people and events . . . Telling his sister—harsh in voice and rude of phrase—to stay where she was, with a sudden access of strength he had thrust aside one or two that hindered him, and leaving the house of Simon the leper had pushed his way, alone, through the crowded streets of Bethany, and now was no more than half a mile from Jerusalem. So much was clear and uncomplicated : and the strength that had come to him was an immediate sequel to an admission he had made. Not to the other people in the room, but only to himself. The admission that now he hated Jesus.

Say it and have done with it, he had thought, and in the waiting ear of his mind he had shouted voicelessly, *He is my enemy and I hate him.* At once he had felt relief, and a cold precipitation of the knowledge that this was true. He felt also that his hatred of Jesus was in some way a triumph over the gross beauty of Mary of Magdala. As though she had offered him the tainted splendour of her body, and with a leather whip he had lashed her white lubricity and driven her from him. She had smelt of whoredom, and the spilling of the perfume—good money viciously thrown away—had been the depravity of

90

a woman lost to all shame and prudence, naked for the enactment of her monstrous submission. She had dried his feet with her hair. She had loosened its coils, let fall a blue-black mane that flung a new odour to the room, and bending low she had wiped his feet with the tingling roughness of it. He had let her do it. He had not shrunk from the wiry touch of it, nor from the brutal luxury of her adoration. He had betrayed a spiritual love, the love of Judas his Disciple, for the licence of a harlot. But hatred, and the admission of hatred, defeated them both. He could whip them away from him . . .

And then to those in the outer room he had cast doubt on the sanity of Jesus, and seen in some of their faces a wrinkle of anticipation, a shameful brightening of their eyes. They were more than half-willing to believe him, and find in his accusation the means of escape. He felt a malicious triumph, but also disgust of those who were contributing to it. Tamar had objected, and cried with pain that he must not say such things. But he told her roughly to be quiet, and would not stay to argue with Philip, who was troubled and sternly disapproving. He wanted to get away from them, and in solitude sharpen himself for what he was going to do.

What that was, he now knew. But he still wanted to assure himself that he was acting sensibly and well, so again he reviewed the sequence of events, and everything he remembered served to fortify his intention. It no longer perplexed him that Jesus should have let himself be called the Son of David, or that he had overturned the tables of the money-changers in the Temple. It merely angered him. Such a man was clearly his enemy, and all he did was hostile to common sense and public safety. To common decency as well as common sense, when he showed his liking for a dishevelled harlot in the odour of her trade and the abomination of her hair . . .

With a violent movement, as if driving away an importunate beggar, he got up and ran recklessly downhill to the road.

Two men, belated travellers to Bethany, turned staring at him, and he grew aware of the need for caution. He could not define or explain this need, but he felt that he must now behave very carefully. He had an important task to fulfil, and he dared not excite suspicion. He must go discreetly, showing no emotion, neither hurrying nor looking alert and self-important, but walking with a casual air, like a man strolling idly and for pleasure. And thus guarded by a front of innocence he would come safely to the Sanhedrin, and tell them what he had learnt.

Eyes were watching him, glinting jelly under black brows, but they could not guess what he knew nor divine his purpose. Inwardly he laughed, but outwardly maintained a demeanour calm and easy. He was perfectly safe, but he must be careful. He walked slowly, and looked about him as though he had no interest in his destination, but merely in what he saw by the wayside.

At the gate into the city there were beggars sitting on either hand. He felt in his pocket to give them a penny, but thought better of it, and for a few yards walked more quickly till he was out of earshot of their disappointed cries.

It would not do, he thought, to go straight to the Sanhedrin. That would be too obvious, for many people knew him by sight and might be watching him. He must take a devious road, and still beneath a mask of carelessness be cautious. He turned into a cobbled lane that led uphill and twisted round a corner.

There was an atmosphere of quiet uneasiness in the city. There were a few people in the streets, and when he came to one of the smaller bazaar districts he was somewhat taken aback to find that none of the stalls was open. The bazaar was deserted except for a pair of loiterers and a group of noisy children. He turned away from it, and took another road.

It led him up a short steep hill and down again. It was narrow, turning between high walls. He rubbed his fingers along the roughness of the wall, and looking over his shoulder grew uneasily aware of the emptiness of the lane behind him. The sun was overhead and the motionless air was hot.

He heard a voice, speaking loudly, and a murmur of other voices that was gently magnified by surrounding walls. He looked into a ruined court, of which the outer wall was broken down, and saw a little crowd of some forty or fifty people to whom a fat black-bearded man was talking excitedly. He stopped to listen, but as though his ears were out-of-tune to human speech, he could make no sense of what he heard.

And then the speaker saw him, and stopped short in the middle of a sentence. His audience turned, not altogether, but one at a time or in sullen groups, and stared at him. Their faces were wary and ill-tempered. They resented his presence, and from some of them came little notes of protest that together sounded like a low-pitched growl. Judas took a step or two backwards, out of the court, and went hurriedly back in the direction from which he had come. A little way along the narrow lane he nearly ran into two men.

He felt a shock of small discomfort when he saw them, and they, also confused, for a moment or two did not know what to say. They were the men—the one crop-eared, the other red-nosed—who had fallen into conversation with him on the road to Bethany.

Then Crop-ear, the first to recover himself, said blandly, 'Well, fancy meeting you again!'

'Just fancy!' added Red Nose.

Judas fingered his mouth and looked from one to the other.

'That was a low-down dirty trick you played,' said Crop-ear, 'when you set Barabbas and his gang against us. We hadn't done you any harm, had we?'

'It had nothing to do with me,' exclaimed Judas. 'I didn't say anything. I didn't tell them to interfere with you.'

'No?'

'No. And I can't stay here——'

'All right, all right, but what's your hurry?'

'Get out of my way!'

'Take it easy,' said Red Nose.

He and Crop-ear stood side by side, and in the narrow high-walled lane there was little room to pass. 'This morning,' said Red Nose, 'I got a poke in the guts that made me cat my heart out.'

Judas tried to thrust his way between them, but Crop-ear pushed him back and said in a surly tone, 'You can't behave like that and get away with it.'

'Don't touch me!' shouted Judas. His voice was hoarse and high, like a peacock screaming, and his opponents, startled by its vehemence, yielded a little ground. Before they could move again there came an answering shout, and round a corner of the lane, twenty yards behind them, appeared half a dozen men, running. Barabbas and the tanner were in the lead.

Crop-ear, braver than his companion, swore angrily when he saw them; but Red Nose, hoarsely exclaiming, took him by the sleeve to start him into flight. For a moment they stood, divided in counsel and the tanner shouted to Judas to hold them. Then Crop-ear's courage failed him, and with Red Nose a yard or two in front, he took to his heels. Neither of them paid any more attention to Judas, who, his back pressed against the wall, kept out of their way.

Barabbas and the tanner followed them; running heavily, breathing loudly. The tanner cried something that was meant to be of comfort as they passed. Behind them, their faces taut with effort, came Simon the pedlar; lantern-jawed, hook-nosed Cushi; a tall pale-cheeked man who ran clumsily because he had only one arm; and Amplias, bright with sweat and out of breath already.

His paces dwindling to a halt, Amplias bent to relieve the pain in his side, and gasping said, 'We've been watching those fellows. They've been trailing you, and we've been trailing them. Josias of Cana—that's him with the one arm—told us who they were. They're spies for the police.'

'They've been following me?'

'Ever since you left Bethany. Didn't you know? We thought from the way you were acting that you had your suspicion of something, and knowing who they were we decided to keep an eye on them. Just in case they got nasty again. Now what's going on along there? Come on, we'll go and see.'

Hurrying past the ruined court from which Judas had retreated, Crop-ear had recognized the black-bearded man who harangued the surly company there, and dragging Red Nose with him, ran in to find a hiding-place among the crowd. A moment or two later Barabbas and the tanner appeared in the broken doorway, followed by Cushi and Simon the pedlar and one-armed Josias. They stood there, breathing heavily, not quite knowing what they should do next. The crowd, turning away from the speaker, stared at them in glum surprise.

'What do you want here?' shouted the black-bearded man. 'If you've come to listen, come in and behave yourselves. If you don't want to listen get to hell out of it.'

'A couple of men just came in here,' said the tanner. 'We want them. They're spies.'

There was a murmur from the crowd, and a movement in the midst of it that began to encircle, to stretch inquiring hands toward Crop-ear and Red Nose.

'Leave them alone!' shouted Blackbeard. 'They're all right. I know who they are, they're friends of mine.'

Josias of Cana pushed his way to the front. 'And who are you?' he asked.

'Is that any business of yours?'

'It may be everybody's business. Your name's Jephthah, isn't it? Well, that's what it used to be. And you're employed by the police, just like those other two.'

'That's a lie!'

Some of the crowd, immediately convinced, began noisily to threaten Jephthah. Crop-ear and Red Nose were roughly handled. A furiously excited foxy-looking man took Josias of Cana by the coat and shouted that Jesus was an agent of the Procurator. Jesus of Nazareth was a traitor to the people.

Josias called to the tanner, 'Come and listen to this.'

'He's being paid by Rome!' shouted the foxy-looking man. 'Jesus was sent here to stir up trouble, so that Rome could step in and grab everything. He's the worst enemy we've ever had!'

'Is that what Jephthah's been telling you?'

'Yes, and he proved it too. He's got proof of everything he says. He saw the Procurator giving money to Jesus.'

Jephthah had been standing on some fallen masonry. He got down and came through the crowd towards them. He was a big man, and unafraid. He said to Josias and the tanner: 'You keep out of this. I'm giving you fair warning, and God help you if you don't take it.'

'You bloody stool-pigeon,' said the tanner.

The foxy-looking man bent suddenly to the ground, and took a brick in his hand; but before he could rise the tanner kicked him in the face and toppled him over. Jephthah swung a short heavy stick that he carried, and hit Josias of Cana on the side of his head. It was on his armless side that he struck him. Then Barabbas pushed forward and tried to grapple with Jephthah, but Jephthah struck again and Barabbas, guarding his head, took the blow on his left forearm. At the same moment he drew a knife from his belt, and closing with Jephthah stabbed him in the belly.

Clutching the wound, Jephthah retreated a few steps, slowly and with failing legs.

The crowd gave way. They forgot their lesser disputing, and turned suddenly quiet and still. With indrawn breath, with fierce and apprehensive interest, they watched Barabbas and the wounded man.

Jephthah tried to straighten himself, and half-lifted

97

D

his cudgel. He took a tottering step forward, but he could not keep his head up. His chin sank, spreading his black beard on his chest, and his knees were loosened. He fell heavily to the ground. Barabbas bent over him and cleaned his knife on the dead man's sleeve.

Then he stood up and said, 'That's the beginning, whether you like it or not. Are we going on with it?'

'We've got to,' said the tanner. 'Where are those two spies?'

About half the crowd, frightened by the killing, had already gone or were hurrying away. Crop-ear and Red Nose had vanished with them.

'And what's happened to Judas?'

'Amplias is looking after him,' said Cushi.

'We ought to hurry,' said Josias. He wiped blood from his head, where Jephthah's blow had torn the scalp, and looked thoughtfully at his reddened hand. 'We've got to separate, and leave word at all the different places, and meet again at the inn.'

'You're going to start it?' asked Cushi.

'As soon as we can.'

'It's got to start some time,' said the tanner.

'But suppose it interferes with his plans? Jesus, I mean?'

'It looks like his advisers are telling him to go slow. Well, that's no good to us. We'll start it, and then he can take command.'

'You're making the hell of a mistake,' said Simon the pedlar. 'I've said from the beginning that violence wouldn't help you. Violence won't do you any good unless you've got solidarity, and knowing the working classes as I do, I say you never will get solidarity. You're just going to walk into trouble blindfold.'

'If you don't want to stay with us, you needn't,'

98

said the tanner. 'We don't want anyone that's half-hearted.'

'Oh, I'm staying,' said Simon. 'I think you're a pack of bloody fools, but the rest of the world's a pack of bloody knaves, so there isn't much choosing.'

'What about them?' asked Barabbas, pointing to the remnant of the crowd that Jephthah had been addressing.

The tanner turned and shouted, 'Are you for us or against us?'

'What are you going to do?' asked one of them.

'Fight,' said the tanner.

'For national freedom, and social justice, and the Kingdom of Christ,' said Josias of Cana, and lifted his one arm in a brave ungainly gesture.

5

Following the others, Judas and Amplias had entered the court a minute or two before the killing of Jephthah. Amplias, eager to see what was happening, pulled Judas into the crowd.

The contagion of anger terrified and bewildered Judas, but when, between two shoulders, he saw Jephthah sagging to fall, his fear was resolved, and became a simple imperative to escape. As soon as the outer fringe of the crowd wavered and turned, he fled with it. With half a dozen others, white-faced as he was, he hurried down the lane. He heard Amplias calling to him, but he did not stop. The Greek went the other way and lost him. Then, looking over his shoulder, Judas caught a glimpse of Crop-ear and Red Nose. They had left the court a little behind him, and were coming the same way.

He ran faster, and fear made him cunning. The lane curved sharply to the right, and round the corner an alley opened in which, behind a heap of straw and dung, stood an open door. He looked back and saw no one. He had drawn ahead of the crowd. He ran down the alley, and into the stable, and shut the door.

In a far corner he stood listening, but heard nothing save the beating of his heart. Slowly that grew quieter and utter silence surrounded him. It was so exquisite after the noise of anger that he was reluctant to move and break it. He stayed in the stable for a long time, till the light that shone, a bluish vapour, through the cracks of the door, and quivered against the darkness, shrank and grew dimmer and left total blackness. Then he nerved himself to go, and with timorous caution, a pulse in his neck half-choking him, he opened as softly as he could the creaking door, and tiptoed into the dusky alley.

There was no one there, but the shadows were full of terror. He walked swiftly away, and grew faint with fear when he saw, dark and unrecognizable beneath the night, an approaching figure. But no one spoke to him, and in a broader thoroughfare a little confidence returned to him.

He was going home. He had abandoned, he had almost forgotten, his mission to the Sanhedrin. That could wait for another day. He thought only of gaining the security of his own house, and shutting the doors against murder, and the spies who sought him, and the populous dark.

THURSDAY

1

BARAK the steward was waiting under the tree in the courtyard. He had been told that Judas was going to the palace of the High Priest, and wanted his company; and knowing how unsettled the city had been, he found the request unsurprising. For his own comfort he had ordered the porter who usually went to the bazaar with him—a burly black-faced fellow—to follow them.

He had hardly spoken to Judas since their quarrel over the beggars' basket, but he knew his master too well to remember such a useless grudge against him; and Judas had forgotten the matter entirely.

They left the house, walking rather too quickly for Barak's comfort. The streets were full of people, townsfolk and the multitude of country-dwellers who had come to celebrate the Passover. They were different from the excited crowds who, throughout the week, had thronged the Temple and the road to Bethany. In a subtle but quite obvious manner they had altered overnight. Their demeanour was lively enough, but now without strain, without self-consciousness. They had put away doubt and self-questioning and revolutionary ardour, and were happy in a traditional fervour and the devotion they had learnt in childhood. When night fell they would eat the lamb they had sacrificed, the bitter herbs of remembrance, and drink the wine of a never-to-be-forgotten deliverance; and against this fixation of the general will—in which patriotism and God and the habit of centuries lay like flies in amber—all new and revolutionary ideas were belittled and almost forgotten. Jesus himself would do nothing to-day, but in the evening, with his own people, would share their devotion and subscribe to ritual. Between days of violence and anxiety, it was a day of peace.

Judas and Barak went more slowly. It was almost impossible to walk quickly among so many people, and Judas, susceptible to the air of peace, grew easier in his mind and felt the need of hurrying diminish. But his intention was unchanged. He was going to tell the Sanhedrin where Jesus could be found, and offer to help in arresting him. His determination was complete, but still he fed it with remembered pictures of Mary stooped in her monstrous adoration, and money rolling on the floors of the Temple, and Jephthah falling with death in his belly. The need to betray him had become an obsession, but as if he doubted its stability—it had been born too suddenly, precipitated by a sudden hatred out of a ferment of emotions—he continued to nourish and fortify it; and against older memories covered the face of Jesus with the harlot's wiry hair.

Barak, more comfortable as their pace grew slower, began to talk. He was a friendly and loquacious man, a little pompous in his style, as befitted an upper servant.

'Have you heard about the rioting last night, sir?' he asked. 'A very nasty affair, I believe, and it might have been much worse if the authorities hadn't got warning in time. There was a regular plot, it seems. A man called Josias, one of those Zealots—he came from

Cana in Galilee—was at the back of it, and another of the leaders was Barabbas, who's well known as a dangerous character. It seems their idea was that if they started an out-and-out rebellion, Jesus would have to put himself at the head of it. They wanted to force his hand, so to speak. But it came to nothing, of course, because the people didn't join in, as they had hoped.

'Or not many, to be accurate. They had more sense, if you ask my opinion. There was a good deal of looting—Barabbas saw to that, I suppose—and finally there was a sort of battle, not far from the Fort. They hadn't a chance, of course, because our soldiers were all ready, and a Roman detachment took them in the rear. Josias was killed, and an old man called Zadok, and about a dozen more, but most of them surrendered. Barabbas put up a good fight, so I heard, but they got him too, and I wouldn't offer much for his chance of life, with him being a deserter from Roman service, and so well known for giving trouble . . .'

These were his late associates, the followers of Jesus and his own companions, thought Judas as he listened to Barak's gossiping story. In his folly he had befriended ruffians and swordsmen, and laboured for the rabble that would turn and destroy him. It was only in the hearts of reckless men that the teaching of Jesus had found earth, and there it had grown to a fearful shape. Men dangerous by their poverty, and the wild hopes that leanness nurtured, had listened to his words, and now Jesus listened to them. And each had made the other mad. A promise of fatness had enraged the poor, the prospect of glory had swept him off his feet. Now both were dangerous, and between them peace would be murdered like

Jephthah with the knife in his belly. He must hurry—
he lengthened his steps again—and put himself and
his knowledge at the service of authority, in the em-
ployment of benignant law.

All these people who filled the streets, mild and
defenceless in their lives, were in danger now, and
he could save them. Perhaps he alone. They were
alive, and life was sacred. He felt his love reaching
out to them as though they were part of his own body,
and dear to him as his own flesh. They were one
people, and God would be in their hearts to-night, and
no doctrine was worth the shedding of their blood.

They came to the palace of the High Priest, and
Judas went in. He waited for a long time in a little
room, and the emotion he had felt for the people in
the streets caressed him. Love, unbidden, had wakened
in him because they had been so orderly, peaceable
in their mien, and happy. He had felt their precarious
tenure of life, and as so often before his heart had
grown large with pity and an aching desire to protect
them. They were lovely in their weakness, in their
docile habit, and at any cost their tenuous happiness
must be preserved. He came near to weeping, but
whether for himself or all humanity he did not know.
And when the pain of his love grew less, he began
to regard it with some complacency. It was laudable,
there was nobility in such love. It gave him another
reason, most cogent of all—his prime reason he
thought now—for betraying Jesus. For that betrayal
would serve and save the humble decent multitude
through which he had been walking. He saw himself
as the saviour of the people.

A servant looked into the little room and went away
again. Then Caiaphas came in. His manner was
friendly, and he behaved as if Judas was a familiar

visitor. He spoke of Cyborea, and regretted that he had not seen her lately.

Judas interrupted him and said, 'I can tell you where Jesus will be to-night.'

Caiaphas stared at him, and appeared to be somewhat embarrassed. 'Oh yes,' he said, 'that will be useful. Very useful. Your uncle will be so glad to hear of your decision. We shall all be grateful. Your uncle is with the Procurator at present——'

'He and the Twelve,' said Judas, 'will be at the inn kept by Elias, a Nazarene, under Herod's Wall——'

'I think,' said Caiaphas, 'that you had better wait till we see the Council, and that will save you telling your story twice. As a matter of fact the Council is sitting now—or rather the Executive Committee of the Council—but we can't do very much for the moment because neither Annas nor your uncle are there. The others were talking rather aimlessly, I thought, so I left them for a little while. Annas and your uncle have gone to see the Procurator again. But they won't do any good, I'm afraid.'

He sat down and looked at his fingers. 'Your mother's well, you said? I'm so glad. I have a great admiration for Cyborea.'

'When do you expect Annas and my Uncle Phanuel to be back?'

'It's very difficult to say. It depends so much on the Procurator, who's quite capable of keeping them waiting for an hour or more. I've had to change my mind about Pilate. I rather liked him at one time, but lately I've come to the conclusion that I was mistaken in him. He's a pushing fellow, and not quite scrupulous, I'm afraid. Do you know him at all?'

'No.'

'I'm disappointed in him. A man of shoddy character, I think. One of those strenuous self-centred people of whom there are so many in the Roman world. No, I don't like him, and I'm very grateful to your uncle, and to Annas as well, for undertaking such a thankless task as asking him for a favour.'

Judas did not reply, and Caiaphas looked round the room with an expression that was half boredom and half anxiety. 'I ought to get back to the Council,' he said. But did not go.

'And your sister?' he asked. 'How is she?'

'She's quite well.'

'A handsome girl, and so like your mother. Your father was a great friend of mine, you know. His death was an irreparable loss. Quite irreparable.'

There was another silence, and Caiaphas said again, 'I really must go. It's just possible that someone has made a useful suggestion. I doubt it, but I suppose it's possible. I'll let you know as soon as Phanuel and Annas have returned, and then you'll come and give us your information? That will be so helpful. You'll forgive me for leaving you alone again? Public affairs have no mercy on a man, none whatever.'

No sooner had Caiaphas gone than Judas wished he had behaved more amiably towards him. Caiaphas had been friendliness itself. He had met Judas as an equal, as a man eager not only to proclaim friendship, but to receive it. He was a lonely man perhaps, and visibly worried . . . Judas felt his love for all weak and docile beings spread farther and embrace the High Priest. But he was restless now, and impatient to be called.

He had to wait another hour, and then a servant conducted him to the Council chamber. In addition to Caiaphas there were twelve members of committee, and most of them were old, grey-bearded, fatly self-important or leanly querulous. He recognized some of them as men whom he had long despised, and in spite of his absorbing impatience he felt a contemptuous surprise at seeing them there.

Phanuel came forward and greeted him, but rather sourly. He and Annas had made no impression on the Procurator, and they were out of humour.

'So you've taken my advice at last?' he said. 'I don't know why you were so stubborn about it. You might have saved us a lot of trouble if you had come a little earlier.'

Caiaphas intervened: 'I should prefer to put it that Judas has come in the nick of time. Every other plan has failed. Annas and Phanuel have failed—through no fault of their own, of course—to move the Procurator from his egotistical position. And now when we are in complete despair Judas has come to our assistance, motivated only by public spirit, and I feel sure that I am speaking for everyone here when I say that we are deeply grateful to him.'

Irritated by the reference to his recent failure, Phanuel muttered to his neighbour, 'It's a pity that his public spirit didn't come to life a couple of days ago.'

The Councillors were looking curiously at Judas, and he, reading their thoughts, grew angry with their lack of understanding, their dull complacency and duller ridicule. He had overheard, or half-heard and half-guessed, his uncle's comment, and hotly resented it. His uncle who had badgered and bewildered him with talk . . .

Annas, ill-temper in every line of his face, said harshly, 'We've wasted enough time to-day, let's waste no more. What have you got to tell us?'

They were putting him into a false position, thought Judas. Only Caiaphas sympathized with him. The others looked on him as if he were a prisoner. Not as the saviour of his people, but as a fool or a criminal. And so he must justify himself. He must explain his conduct, and tell then how wrong they were, how lofty were his motives, how noble his intention. And something, perhaps, of what he had suffered . . .

'Come on,' said Annas. 'Speak up.'

'I have nothing to be ashamed of,' declared Judas loudly. 'In all I have done I have been moved by the desire to help those who were less happy than myself, and to assist in a revaluation of our common faith. That, as I understood it, was the declared mission of Jesus of Nazareth. I do not regret my association with him. If he had confined his teaching, as he began it, to exposition of our common need for charity and the loving-kindness of our Father in Heaven, I should be his disciple still. But recently, yielding I suppose to the influence of those about him, he has let people take an immoderate view of his authority, and in my opinion——'

'My dear boy,' interrupted Phanuel, 'I'm sure your opinions are very interesting, but as time is pressing we'd rather hear your news. Where is Jesus going tonight, and how many people will be with him?'

'I think,' said Caiaphas, 'that Judas might be allowed to tell his story in his own way.'

Annas, watching Judas closely, growled, 'Yes. Let him alone. Go on, boy.'

Phanuel shrugged his shoulders, and Judas tried to gather his words again into the groove where they had been running. But the interruption had disordered his thought, and he could not redirect it. He hesitated, stammered a little, and then cried, 'I came here to save the people. To save them from violence and the poverty of war, and death in the streets. Not out of hatred for him, but love of my own people . . .'

His words dried and disappeared like a trickle of water in the sand. He had forgotten his hatred till his voice, denying it, reminded him. And now he could not quite remember how it had been born. He rubbed his eyes, and against the red background of their lids saw the stooping figure of Mary of Magdala. That was it. That and the wasting of things. Despising things, because he was superior to them. The spilling of perfume, and money on the floor, like slipping a knife into a man's side to spill for wantonness the blood that kept him alive. That was the reason for his hating Jesus, but suddenly he grew too tired to think about it. Hatred was so heavy a burden.

Annas got up and came towards Judas, and stood in front of him. 'We've listened to your motive,' he said, 'and no one here has any quarrel with it. Now for your information.'

'When my uncle first came to speak to me about this,' said Judas slowly, 'he promised that Jesus wouldn't be arrested on a criminal charge, but simply taken into custody for his own safety.'

'That was three days ago!' shouted Phanuel. 'Things have changed a lot since then. I warned you, but you wouldn't take my warning, and it's too late now to ask for leniency and special terms.'

'Then I won't do it. I won't tell you.'

To the man who sat next him Caiaphas whispered, 'As a matter of fact he has told me already, and do you know, for the life of me I can't remember what he did tell me?'

Annas, staring closely at Judas, his large and wrinkled face savage in the midst of his beard, growled at him, 'You're trying our patience, you're trying it too far.'

Shrinking from the threat of his discoloured cheeks, Judas hugged the wall with his shoulder-blades. Annas, in the same deep vibrant voice, went on: 'You'd better make up your mind and tell us what you know. You've come too far to retreat now. You're not going to leave here till you do tell us. And the sooner the better. The sooner you tell us the sooner you can go . . .'

The menace of his voice and the reiterated intimidation of his words were unnerving, and Judas said weakly, 'Go to the inn kept by Elias of Nazareth under Herod's Wall, by the road to Gethsemane. That's where he'll be.'

'Who are going to be with him?'

'The Twelve.'

'Including you?'

'I said I would be there.'

'Is he spending the night there?'

'I don't think so.'

'Then where is he going?'

'I don't know.'

Annas turned to the Council and said, 'We've got our chance. He and his so-called Disciples are going to this inn, under Herod's Wall, and they might as well be in the desert of Jeruel. Every street will be empty, every man indoors. We'll surround the inn, arrest the lot of them, and have them all in custody without a soul knowing it.'

One of the Council, an old man with a deep but quavering voice, said in surprise, 'But surely they also will be celebrating the Passover?'

'I suppose so.'

'Then you can't arrest them in the middle of their meal.'

'Why not?'

'It would be sacrilege!'

From the other Councillors came a muttering of agreement. Some of them had been profoundly shocked by Annas's suggestion, and none liked it. If it became known that they had torn a man from the ritual feast, the whole people might turn against them. Such was the argument of some, and others objected to the plan because they were horrified by its impiety. Annas protested, and roughly maintained a case for expediency. Often, he said, there was more morality in being expedient than in lying fettered to the dead wood of the pandects. This brought to their feet in fury all the Pharisees on the Council, and Annas was forced to retract. His dark face twitching with temper, he sat down, and in a surly voice exclaimed: 'Then make your own plans! I've shown you a way out of your difficulty, and if you won't take it, you'll have to find another for yourselves.'

'If Judas takes the meal with them,' said Phanuel, 'he can easily question them and discover where they are going afterwards. He can make some excuse and leave the inn——'

'No,' said Judas, 'I've done enough.'

'Indeed you have done a great deal,' said Caiaphas. 'You have done more than anyone could expect you to do, and again I should like to assure you of our gratitude. Come and sit down, and let us talk this over.—There's no reason why he should stand, is there?—I remember once, when I was with your father, being very much impressed by something he said, I can't recall his words precisely, but the gist of them was that persistence in well-doing was more

111

important than being successful in well-doing. A very profound and searching criticism. And I was equally impressed, a few minutes ago, by what you said about the motives that induced you to associate with Jesus. Again I've forgotten your exact words, but they showed quite clearly, I think, that all your life you have delighted in the thought of public service. Well, that's most admirable, especially in a young man. And now I am coming to the point, and that is that you must remember what your father said about the all-importance of being persistent. You mustn't give up your good work because of a passing weariness. You mustn't forget that you have it in your power to help us all. To help the whole nation, in fact. You, and you alone, are in the position to give us information that will enable us to deal with this perplexing difficulty in a peaceful manner. Without bloodshed, without more rioting. Now won't you think again, and consider from this wider aspect the suggestion that Phanuel has made? . . .'

Caiaphas understood him. Caiaphas realized his lofty motive. Like a hand in the darkness, the sympathy of Caiaphas came out to find him; and eagerly he took it. He would do whatever they wished, he said. He would give them all the help in his power. He repeated this, for at the first saying he had tripped and stumbled among the words. But now they came more easily.

He told them how he enjoyed the confidence of the Twelve, and kept the purse for them. His words ran like a river in the spring, bridge-high with mountain-snow and tumbling to the sea. He described his feelings when, in the morning, he had found himself in the midst of the people, and seen their danger and realized his love. He refrained with difficulty from announcing himself as their saviour. For some obscure and shapeless reason he felt that such an avowal would be unwise. Some of the Councillors were already whispering.

2

His hidden knowledge filled him full. It plumped his skin and made his legs strong. In his mind he kept turning over and over, as if caressing it with his hands, the secret fact of his significance. He was the saviour of the people, working alone, his purpose close-guarded. In the cup of his hands lay the Sanhedrin, he held the Disciples in his grasp. Sweetly on his tongue lay the memory of the words he had spoken, that promised peace to Jerusalem, and with a dark delight he knew that he could still unsay his promise. No one but himself knew all his power, though Caiaphas was aware of his importance, Caiaphas sympathized with him. But the other members of the Sanhedrin were tedious ineffective old men, old dullards who lived in a caul of thick senility, and Annas was no more than a brute, with the cunning of his kind and its limitations. He would have his revenge on Annas, when his triumph was achieved and recognition came to him for his saving of the community, for unarming war.

The people would hail him in the streets, he would walk in the sunlight of their gratitude. They would say : Like Joshua who bade the day stand still, he held forth his hand and commanded that war should not come upon us. They would turn to bless him, the multitude crying with one voice, Our Saviour !

That would be his reward. He asked nothing more, save the humiliation of Annas. To live in a peace of his own making would be honour and price enough. To walk in the city and see in every passing creature a life he had saved, to hear on every voice a murmur of praise! A sweet intoxicating thought. Sweet also, and sufficient for the moment, was the taut and fleet-foot sensation of power. The inner knowledge, the turning-over of strength, the purpose tip-toe and alert. There were people in the street—but not many now—and no one knew his secret. There a man went hurrying down a lane, a girl called sharply. But neither knew him, nor knew that like God himself he had power to cut their lives to the root, or give them many years that would be lovely with the morning and the evening and the voices of their friends. He was like God, for he had life and death in his hands. But in the houses on either side they were gathering at the table, they were drinking the appointed wine, they would eat the bread of remembrance, yet none might hear his footsteps of mercy. He was like the angel of God, for he could walk invisible through the streets, he was viewless in the gathering dark, a shadow moving with no sound in the fine-spun veil of the twilight. He was all alone . . .

He came to the inn where Jesus and the Disciples were to eat the Supper of the Passover. He was not the last to arrive, for some of the Twelve, alarmed by a rumour that the police were watching their movements, had stayed in the houses of friends till darkness fell. They came in cautiously, and then in the lamplight there was relief on their faces. The inn-keeper was one of their earliest adherents, a Nazarene, and except for him and his relations there was no one else in the house.

Judas looked from one to another of his companions and felt, in a tolerant good-humoured way, contemptuous of them. They were decent well-intentioned people, but of very ordinary intelligence. And they were quite powerless, of course. There was nothing impressive in their appearance, and their speech, when they were talking together in familiar circumstances, was trivial enough. They were all there except Peter and Andrew. Jesus was in another room, speaking to the innkeeper and his family, so Peter and Andrew were probably with him . . .

One of them was saying he was sure he had been followed when he came in the morning from Bethany. That was Thaddeus, an excitable person with quick birdlike movements and a harsh voice. He was talking to the brothers James and John. They were thickset men with deep-tanned faces and strong round shoulders; and they were plainly sceptical. But Simon the Zealot found no difficulty in believing the story. Like enough, he said, they were all being watched. He knew something about the police and their methods, for he had been a revolutionary, open and avowed, for many years. Incitement to rebellion had become a vocation to him, that he practised with unfailing zeal but without much hope. He was cynical as well as earnest, scornful of humanity and with little reverence for himself.

Judas interrupted him. He had never liked Simon, whom he regarded as a professional malcontent. He began to relate his own experience with spies. Yesterday, he said, he had been followed all day by a pair of men whom finally he had eluded by a timely trick. He made a fine boastful story of it, spoke loudly, grew livelier in his narration, and got the attention of all who were in the room.

He felt a warm and bubbling triumph when he saw how intently everyone was listening to him. But he was

115

not surprised. It was so easy for him to dominate these simple men. He could do as he liked with them. And then he saw that Philip was looking at him with a curious expression, and he remembered his indiscretion in Simon the leper's house in Bethany. Philip had been there, and heard him. He made his story gallop, and brought it to an end.

'And for all I know,' he said, 'they're looking for me still. And for all I care, they can go on looking for me. It doesn't worry me.'

Then, to avoid Philip, and also to prove that he could exert his influence over people whom he disliked, and who had little liking for him, he drew Thaddeus and Simon the Zealot into a corner, and wrapped them in his friendship.

'I think we should be safe enough to-night,' said Thaddeus.

'Where are you going? It was early when I left Bethany and nothing had been decided.'

'Do you know the ruins of an old house on the other side of Gethsemane, a little way out of the village? There's an orchard beside it, all overgrown. No one has lived there for years. That's where we are going. It isn't likely that anyone will think of looking for him there.'

'It would be madness to go back to Bethany,' said Simon. 'They'll be watching the road, and watching Bethany too. Even if he got there alive, he wouldn't be safe. Not to-night, with everyone indoors and thinking only of their own affairs. It's the best night in the year for a nice quiet assassination.'

'I wish the next few days were safely over,' said Thaddeus.

'I'd be happy enough if to-night was over.'

116

The innkeeper appeared, bringing the wine. He saw that everyone had arrived, and went out again. A minute or two later, Jesus came in, followed by Peter and Andrew.

Judas felt the blood beat more quickly on his temples. It was like a tiny drum that set his spirit marching, and alone among the Disciples he looked carefree and confident.

3

Making an excuse, Judas left the inn before the others. He stood for a moment or two, and let his eyes grow accustomed to the darkness. The shape of a wall and the flat roof of a house grew more distinct. The night air was cool, and he could see the dim shape of the lane like a canal brimfull of dusky water, the hard outline of its banks. He could still hear voices in the inn.

He went quickly down the lane and turned into the road that led to Gethsemane. Thirty yards in front of him rose the city wall, and beneath it lay a belt of black shadow. He hesitated, peering into the thick darkness, and suddenly he was surrounded by a group of men from whose clothing, as they moved, came the little chink of steel.

A voice, pitched low but with authority in it, asked, 'Is this the man?' And another voice, hoarse and brusque, demanded, 'Judas Iscariot?'

'Yes,' said Judas.

The first voice, speaking rapidly, said, 'My orders are to take you to the Commandment of the Temple Guard. You will give him what information you have, and receive further instructions from him.'

'No!' exclaimed Judas. 'I've done what I said I would do, and I'm free now. I'll tell you where they're going. They're going to Gethsemane, a house on the other side——'

'I'm sorry,' said the officer, 'but my orders were quite definite.'

A soldier took Judas by the arm, seizing him above the elbow. The patrol closed round him, and they turned again into the city.

'Let me go!' said Judas irritably. 'You've no right to treat me like a prisoner.'

'Of course not,' said the officer. 'Leave him alone, sergeant.'

Judas was mollified. The officer had a pleasant voice, and appeared willing to treat him with politeness, if not with respect. He straightened his shoulders, and to assert himself—to show that he was a free man and a person of importance—asked, 'Who are you?'

'My name's Boaz,' said the officer. 'I think I know some of your family. You've cousins in Alexandria, haven't you? I'm a captain in the Tetrarch's First Peraean Regiment.'

'Then what are you doing here?'

'The Temple authorities asked for assistance, and Herod lent them my regiment. We came in last night, after it was dark.'

'I heard nothing of that.'

'No, it was kept pretty secret, of course. We did a very good forced march the night before last.'

Judas felt his importance evaporating a little, and a querulous dissatisfaction coming in to take its place. This massing of forces was unfair to him. It was unnecessary, for he had taken control of the situation.

and could deal with any difficulty. But his glory would be diminished if he must share it with Herod Antipas.

He said angrily, 'They're a lot of fools in the Sanhedrin! There's no danger now. The crisis is practically over, and I can't see any point in bringing in the Tetrarch of Galilee.'

Boaz maintained his easy temper. 'There isn't much danger from Jesus and his followers,' he said. 'I don't think there ever was. The real danger is Rome and Pontius Pilate. If there was anything like serious trouble in Jerusalem, he'd walk in and set up his eagles in the Temple. He'd simply love to see us fighting among ourselves, and personally I think Herod has plenty of justification in doing anything at all to keep Pilate from swallowing us whole.'

But where, cried Judas to himself, was recognition of what he was doing? Boaz said nothing of him, who was the most vital factor in the whole situation. He spoke only of the vague masses that moved, so clumsy and so helpless, on its far periphery. Neither Herod nor the Sanhedrin, but he was the saviour of Jerusalem and all its people. Let the Council deliberate night and day, and soldiers march from Dan to Beersheba, but what could they have done to avert war had he not come forward to show them the way? He and he alone was the corner-stone of peace—and Boaz could not see him . . .

But he must not lay claim to his rights. Not yet. Not till the soldiers had gone and the shadow of war lay underfoot. He must be wary and keep guard over his tongue. Once already he had spoken rashly that evening, when Jesus with a naked look upon his face had said, 'Truly I tell you, one of you is going to betray me.' And before he could check it his wanton tongue had blabbed the silly question, 'Surely it is not me?'—He had heard himself speaking, as though it was another man, aghast at what he had said.—It was true that he had done himself no great harm, for half a dozen others, fear pinching their cheeks, had made the self-same query. But talking was dangerous, that was clear enough, and he must use care till all was safe and he could take his confidence from the open sky. He must go cunningly while darkness lay, and swallow humiliation as best he could.

They came to the Temple barracks, and leaving his patrol outside, Boaz took Judas in, and led the way to the Commandant's room. He saluted, and announced the accomplishment of his mission.

Malchus, the Commandant, was a melancholy man with a big body and a confirmed habit of immobility. He barely acknowledged Boaz's salute, and looked at Judas with no apparent interest.

'What's your information?' he asked.

'I want to see Caiaphas,' said Judas quickly. 'I should prefer to report to him personally, and consult with him as to what ought to be done.'

'There would be no point in you seeing Caiaphas,' answered Malchus in a voice as cold and dull as a wet winter morning. 'The arrangements for the arrest are in my hands.'

'I ask it as a personal favour. Considering my position and what I've done to help you I might claim it as my right. But I merely ask you. I make a request——'

'No,' said Malchus.

Boaz intervened : 'I've already gathered, from conversation with the . . .' He hesitated, and then continued, 'From conversation with Judas Iscariot, that Jesus and his immediate followers will be spending the night in or near the village of Gethsemane.'

'We can surround it, I suppose,' said Malchus.

'And what good would that do you?' cried Judas in a shrill sudden temper. 'You'll never find him without my help. Never! You think I'm in your power, but I'm not. You're in mine, mine! I know what you want to do. A blind man could see it. You want to leave me out of this. You want all the credit for yourself. You want people to think it was you who saved them. But I'm not going to be cheated out of my rights. I know where he is, and you don't, and I'm not going to be left behind while you rob me of what I've worked for and contrived and sweated for. I'm not going to be ignored and cast off. I'm not going to be treated like a nonentity. I'm coming with you, do you hear? I'm coming with you!'

Boaz revealed, clearly enough, a bewildered disliking of this tirade; but Malchus listened to it with no more surprise than might be shown by a little raising of the brows and a look of sombre interest.

'All right,' he said. 'You'll come with us and guide us. When do you think we should start?'

Judas, his eyes dilated, his face ridged with passion, stared at him as if he suspected another trap, and strove to see where it was hidden. Malchus repeated his question: 'When should we start?'

Judas began to laugh. It was a harsh and grating sound, but there was mirth in it. A jeering distorted mirth, and a note of clownish triumph.

'You admit it!' he cried. 'You can't do without me. You admit it, don't you? I know their plans, and you don't so you're in my power, just as much as he is. But you needn't worry, I'll see that you don't make any mistake about it. You follow my advice, and you'll be all right.'

'Good,' said Malchus. 'And what is your advice?'

121

Solemn now, and pondering the question, Judas answered slowly, 'I left the inn as soon as I could. The others weren't ready to go, but I don't think they would stay very long. Some of them were nervous. I think they'll have left by now. And .they haven't far to go. An orchard on the other side of Gethsemane—but I'm not going to tell you were it is! You'll have to take me with you!'

'Of course,' said Malchus.

'And if you'll wait till they're all asleep, you can take them by surprise. Two of them have got swords.'

'Are those all the weapons they have?'

'Yes. They were talking about it. Two swords.'

'That shouldn't give us much trouble.'

'But if you wait till they're asleep——'

'All right,' said Malchus. 'We'll wait for an hour and start then. Will you be quite comfortable if I leave you here? Boaz will stay with you, but I've got some work to do.'

Malchus got up and walked heavily to the door, and Boaz, obviously reluctant, was left with Judas.

4

The soldiers were waiting outside. There were a hundred men of the Tetrarch's Peraean Regiment, and fifty of the Temple troops. They stood in the darkness of the barrack square, talking in low voices, grumbling a little. Under-officers walked to-and-fro.

Boaz and Judas came out, and a little later Malchus followed them. The murmur of talk was silenced, and a voice, clear-cut and imperative, shouted a command, There was the sound of many feet moving together, and the column wheeled out of the square. They left the city and turned north along the road that ran parallel with the brook Kedron. The sky was broken, and there were stars in the ragged gulfs between the clouds.

Gethsemane lay at the intersection of the valley road and the road to Jericho. It was a straggling village, and on the one side there were houses on the rising ground that grew into the Hill of Olives. Two hundred yards short of the cross-roads the column halted, and a couple of scouts came in with the news that all was quiet. A detachment under Boaz was sent off to take up a position north of the village, and a picket line was posted between the village and Jerusalem. The main body then left the road and moved slowly towards the hill.

Presently they halted, and Malchus held a short consultation. Judas had described the house and the adjoining orchard, and he knew its position. It had lain deserted for many years, but it had once been well-tended. It was known as the Garden of Gethsemane. Malchus, with Judas and forty men of the Temple troops, now cautiously advanced towards it.

The ground was rough, the grass grew rank, and the unpruned trees were thick and woody. A man, startled from sleep, rose with a wild cry from the undergrowth, and ran towards the inner part of the orchard. The soldiers, with no further need for silence, advanced more quickly. They heard shouting from the other side, where another of the Disciples had been surprised by their encircling movement. Many of the soldiers carried lanterns, which they had hidden under their cloaks, but now they held them up and from all sides their yellow light shone through the branches of the trees and threw writhing shadows that were lost in the long grass. The Disciples, panic-stricken, fled before them, stumbling as they ran, but could find no escape.

Then their cries were quietened, and in a little square of open ground in the middle of the orchard, Jesus stood up and asked, 'Who is it you are looking for?'

Malchus, panting slightly, said : 'Jesus of Nazareth.'

'I am he.'

Malchus motioned to two of the soldiers who carried lanterns. They went a little nearer and held their lanterns high.

Judas, who had kept close to Malchus, pulled his sleeve to get his attention; but Malchus impatiently thrust him back.

Sore as a wound when the bandage is ripped off, his old suspicion broke raw in Judas's mind. They were trying to keep him out of the picture. They were still hoping to steal the credit for what he had done. They were treating him as a thing of no account, a shabby coat they could throw away when winter had gone . . .

With a hoarse cry, 'Master, Master!' he pushed aside the nearest soldier, and in the midst of the lanterns and the ring of armed men, he threw his arms round Jesus's neck, and kissed him.

Jesus said, 'Are you betraying the Son of Man with a kiss?'

As if the word of treachery had opened his mind to what was happening, the disciple Peter, sobbing in fury, raised his sword and ran at Malchus. But a soldier threw himself in the way, and Peter struck short and feebly. Malchus, immobile as ever, made no perceptible movement till he put his hand to his ear. The wound was trifling, but Peter had drawn blood. Then the soldiers roughly took hold of Jesus and the

Disciples, but Jesus said, 'I have told you who I am. If it is me you are looking for, let these men go away.'

Malchus, frowning at the blood on his hand, said shortly, 'You're the only one I want. The others can go where they please.'

'Day after day,' said Jesus, 'I was in the Temple, and you never stretched a hand against me.'

Malchus shrugged his shoulders, and told an under-officer to get the men back to the road. Whistles blew in the darkness, and the soldiers reassembled. Some of the Disciples fled incontinently, but others surrounded Judas and would have beaten him had not the soldiers come to his rescue.

When they were on the road again, he looked for Boaz, and told him what he had done. He was in a state of much excitement, and was very well pleased with himself. 'There were lanterns all round us,' he said, 'and all the soldiers were watching. I kissed him in front of them all. There could be no mistake about it. I was the one who had arranged everything, and I showed that by kissing him. I was quite right, don't you think? There shouldn't be any doubt about a thing like that.'

Boaz listened to him with great disliking, but said little. He was a kindly young man, and under certain obligations to Judas's cousins, whom he had met in Alexandria. But he wondered whether Judas was losing his sanity.

5

Malchus took his prisoner to the High Priest's palace. The great house was lighted and murmurous with activity. There were torches in the courtyard, and servants hurrying, and in the administrative wing the rooms were illumined and Councillors, hastily summoned, were still arriving. According to Jewish law it was illegal to try for a capital offence at night, nor might anyone be brought to judgment during the time of the Passover. But Jesus was led immediately to a room where Annas waited with the jurists of the Council, proctors and police; and with no other formality than a general assumption of his guilt, they set about to badger him into confessing it.

In the voices of those who questioned him, and Annas's yellow-wrinkled face, there was manifest the urgency of their desire for revenge and to be done with him. They had been afraid of him, and never till now admitted how much afraid. But now they betrayed it in the savage reiteration of their questions, in their voices that were harsh with anger and anxiety. For he was still dangerous. So long as he lived he was a peril to them, and everything on which they had built their lives; but he could not be condemned until they had patched together some ragged evidence of guilt. Of blasphemy, of treason, or both together. So voice after voice assailed him, shouted questions, set traps for him. They gave him no rest.

A clerk came in, tiptoed across the floor, and whispered to Annas. It was his second visit, and the first time Annas had sent him packing. Nervously, with dry lips and a kind of cringing importunacy, he repeated his request. Annas listened impatiently, refused him, and then called him back. 'Wait,' he said.

He turned to Jesus, his eyes wolfish, his mouth working in the yellow-grey thicket of his beard, and with stabbing forefinger shouted: 'You prophesied the destruction of the Temple, that's one charge. You claim to speak in God's holy name, that's another.

And you forbade the people to pay their taxes, and there's a third. Do you or do you not admit these charges?'

Jesus answered wearily, 'I have spoken openly to the world. I have taught in synagogues and in the Temple. I have said nothing in secret. Why ask me? Ask those who heard me. They know what I said.'

A police-officer who stood beside Jesus hit him in the face, and looked with uncertain bravado at the watching jurists. The noise of the blow was sharp and decisive above the murmur of voices.

Annas, breathing hoarsely, said, 'Take him to the High Priest and call your witnesses.' Then to the waiting messenger: 'I'll come and speak to him myself.'

It was Judas, again demanding his rights, who had persuaded a credulous though reluctant clerk that he must be heard. Since the arrival of Malchus and his prisoner at the palace, Judas had been almost completely ignored. It seemed as if no one knew anything about him. He had tried to follow Jesus into the room where Annas was waiting; but a soldier at the door, deaf to appeal, had pushed him away. He had demanded to see Caiaphas, but no one had paid any attention till some minor official, listening with the tetchy boredom of a man who hears too many petitions, had briefly told him he must wait, and showing him into a little empty room, had left him there.

A narrow window overlooked the courtyard, and Judas could hear the chatter of excited servants and the dull repeated fragments of their gossip. He could hear the shrill voice of a girl and the deep frightened words of a man. He looked out and saw, in the ruddy flare of a torch, Peter and a little thin kitchenmaid, all eyes and teeth and gesticulation, who before a dozen of her fellow-servants was shrieking some accusation against him. Judas could not hear what. But whatever it was, Peter, unhappy and afraid, was urgently denying it.

It made Judas angrier than he had already been to find himself still in his old company, and to hear again the loud unrest it so often created. He was sick and tired of all the tedious fishermen and pious tax-collectors he had been living with, and wanted to be finished with them. But not without honour to himself, not without credit for what he had done. He was hungrier than ever for his reward, his belly was pinched with the pains of starvation for it.

He went out and called to a clerk who had stopped to listen with long ears to some distant conversation. He was a meagre fellow, of middle age, his manhood faded, his mind bewildered by the turmoil but avid for every detail of it. He listened to Judas, and believed all he said. But he was afraid of Annas, and needed much persuasion before he would consent to take a message to him.

Judas waited. He began to cry with rage and vexation, but worse than the fighting and the falling holds of impotence was the agony of fear, lest he be cheated of his due, that tore his belly with iron beaks. Then at last Annas came, with the credulous clerk and a dull, short-sighted, elderly man behind him.

Judas, wiping with both hands his tear-stained face, cried in tremulous voice, 'Why was I left here? How can you get on without me? I've got my rights and I'm not going to be overlooked like this. You're still dependent on me!'

'You're getting anxious about your money, are you?' said Annas, and nodded to the elderly man, who, untying the strings of a little leather bag, poured from it a chattering rush of silver coins.

'Thirty?' asked the elderly man.

'Thirty,' said Annas, and grinned like a grey wolf.

'What are you trying to do?'

'I'm paying you,' said Annas, 'for the information you gave us.'

'With money?'

'Of course.'

'But I don't want money! There isn't money enough in the world to pay for what I've done. I saved the people, saved you all. I took everything on my own shoulders, and—how much do you say?'

'Thirty,' said the elderly man.

'Oh, damn you, damn you!—No, don't go! You can't cheat and swindle me and leave me no chance to explain! You don't understand, you've no glimpse of the hell I've gone through, and all I've done for you. You've got peace now, and who gave it to you? There are people asleep now, safe and sleeping in every house in the city, and who stopped them dreaming of blood and the Romans coming? I did. I did! I knew how to do it, when you were helpless, and now you try to pay me with the price of a slave. If you gave me all the treasure of the Temple——'

'You won't get a penny more,' said Annas. 'And you needn't think we're under any further obligation to you.'

'You'll hear the children shouting it! In every street of the city you'll hear my name, and gratitude for the bread they eat in peace because I gave them peace. I put out my hand, and war stood still—and you think you can pay me with thirty pieces of silver and discharge your debt? You chousing corruption of

129

E

a fox, rotten to the heart—don't go, don't go! No, Annas, let me explain, you don't understand. Let me tell you what I've done!'

'You were a useful informer,' said Annas, 'and you have been paid for your trouble. I have no further interest in you.'

Shouting incoherently, Judas clung to him, but the frightened clerk and the elderly man from the Treasury pulled him away, and Annas, his bitter calm a little shaken, went hurriedly from the room.

Judas was left alone. 'Fox, you reasty fox!' he cried against the blankness of the door. 'Bred like a dog in the street, dropped in a laystall, you dung-tail cogging thief! Come back, come back!—No, stay, stay and drink your spittle and be poisoned. The pox blind you and hell find you! Take your money, take your dead eyes and buy scabs for your sores. God damn you and give me revenge! Give me revenge to trample you home in the muck of the shambleyard. I'll tell them yet, they'll cry me through the streets and run to kiss the hem of my cloak and lift their eyes in my shadow and curse you till the fire of universal hatred cracks through your bones and your belly founders and pariah dogs fight for your pluck in the gutter! Take your dead eyes and count your leprosy in hell. Oh, damn you past all remembrance!'

He scrambled on the floor, gathered another fistful of the money he had knocked from the hand of the old short-sighted man, and flung it against the door. Panting, he grovelled and looked for more, but suddenly collapsed and lay sobbing. His legs were twitching, and his shoulders rose and fell like a man convulsive under the whip.

When he got up there was a loose and bewildered look on his face, and tears and the dust of the floor had begrimed his cheeks. He stood for a minute, swaying slightly, uncertain what to do. The money lay on the floor, white pieces like the upturned sightless eyes of beggars in the shadow of a wall. Like patches of leprosy under the darkness of a sleeve. He rubbed his eyes, and looked quickly over his shoulder. There was no one there.

He knelt, and gathered a dozen coins, and crawled round the room looking for more. When he had found them all he sat down and spread them on a table and began to count them . . .

Twenty-six, twenty-seven, twenty-eight, twenty-nine. There was one short. He looked for it, and could not find it. He counted them again, but lost his tally in the middle. He could not make thirty of them. He laid them in rows of five, but his sleeve brushed a coin to the floor, and again he was wrong. He stared at them, suspicious and perplexed.

He heard footsteps outside the door, and sweeping the coins together, stuffed them into a pocket. He stood up and waited; but no one came in. Slowly a look of cunning tightened the looseness of his face, and gave him a semblance of wary composure. He patted his coat where the silver lay, and listened to the chink of the coins. Then he opened the door and peered out. The passage was empty. Cautiously he went out, holding his heavy pocket to keep the money quiet. He came into the courtyard, and through the dark streets hurried home.

FRIDAY

1

THERE was no longer any concealment of the soldiers, in their barracks or the Fort, but now they were to be seen on all sides, and filled the city with a general threat. Jewish and Roman, they patrolled the streets and guarded cross-roads. With clank of armour they marched from the Fort, and with a clatter of ironshod butts they grounded their spears before the Temple. There was no means of escaping them, nor of forgetting the menace they carried on their weapons and in their cold inhuman discipline.

Before daybreak the news had gone through the city that Jesus had been arrested. It had spread like flood-water when a dam has broken, here rushing in a thin far-reaching wave, there channelling more slowly, more circuitously, but always advancing. It had brought people from their beds, from bakehouse and loom, from smithy and stable and the wells where women, shivering in the dawn, waited their turn. It was told like news of war, a husband's death. It was whispered by cold lips, and cried in sudden terror to the darkness beyond a half-open door. It drove away all other thoughts, and left silence behind it. Men stood appalled, their bodies hollow with dismay, and women, crouched upon their stools, hid their faces. Then slowly and by ones and twos they came into the streets, and looking for comfort in their neighbours' faces, saw calamity and shame. They saw the soldiers standing, leaning on their spears, and read the menace in their eyes.

Like ghosts uncertain of the way, they turned hesitantly towards the palace of the High Priest, and presently in a sort of panic began to run. Then the soldiers checked them, and broke their mass. They scattered, and a whisper met them that Jesus had been taken before Pilate, to the Praetorium. They turned in that direction, leaning quickly into narrow lanes, swooping to avoid a square-fronted Roman patrol. Wheeling as plovers in a gale, dividing and circling the sky and coming together again, from alleys and twisting thoroughfares they entered the great square before the Praetorium.

The building itself was guarded by Roman troops, but Temple soldiers kept order in the crowd. The square was full of people, but few could see what was going on, or hear what was said. So their silence lifted, with the last coldness of night, and as if life and heat were returning to their blood they craned and called to their neighbours to ask what was happening. They fell quiet for a minute, and again their voices met in a harsh and murmuring stream that flowed from side to side.

On perjured and conflicting evidence the Sanhedrin had found Jesus guilty of blasphemy, and pronounced sentence of death, But still they were afraid of the people, and again they were trying to persuade Pilate to take responsibility from their shoulders, and put the sentence into execution with Roman hands, Before Pilate they arraigned Jesus on other charges, of sedition and high treason. But the Procurator was as cunning as the Council. They could stir the pot themselves, since only trouble would come to the surface. If Jesus was a king, where was his kingdom? In a realm that gave no profit to Pilate, paid no revenue to Caesar. The kingdom of truth—and what

133

was truth? He could rule if he cared in such a moon-lit land. Not guilty of treason.

'Not guilty! Not guilty!' The voices roared in the square, and the soldiers turned savagely against them.

And as to sedition, said Pilate, as to his unruly preaching in the north, why not take him to Herod? Jesus was a Galilean, wasn't he? Well, Herod Antipas was in Jerusalem—he had come for the Passover—and Herod was Tetrarch of Galilee. Herod was the man to deal with one of his own subjects on a charge like that.

The priests were furious, half-inarticulate with rage. Pilate obdurate, a cunning triumph in his eyes. Caiaphas made helpless gestures, but Annas between his teeth said, 'Take him to Herod.' The crowd followed, clamorous and surging like a many-pointed sea against the line of soldiers.

Herod saw Jesus, laughed and commanded him to perform a miracle or two. But Jesus was not the only one he mocked. He laughed at the priests, and refused to pull chestnuts out of the fire for them. The priests chattered like apes at sunset, but Jesus was silent. Then the Tetrarch, laughing still, gave Jesus a purple gown, and bade them take him back to Pilate. The multitude were bewildered when they saw Jesus in the colour of royalty, and some, misled by a glimpse of splendour and ever hopeful, raised a shout: 'Hail! Hail the Son of David!' But the soldiers of the Temple, thrusting through the crowd, beat them cruelly into silence.

Again they filled the square before the Praetorium and innumerable voices made a thickness in the air, as of midges above a stagnant pool. The sun was over the house-tops, and in its warmth rose the smell of poverty. But now there was division in the crowd, and many were siding with the priests and saying that Jesus should be put to death. A shout went up, 'Crucify him!' It was repeated here and there, provocatively in places, elsewhere in new-kindled rage and hatred. The soldiers made no attempt to silence the shouting. Some of those who demanded crucifixion were agents of the Sanhedrin. Others were small traders whose livelihood depended on priestly favour, and a good many were simple people who had been frightened by rumours that Jesus mean to destroy the Temple and perhaps the city as well. As soon as they heard the cry for blood their fear and hatred found expression, and they added their smouldering passion to an uproar that had been coldly organized.

Brawling began, and people were thrown to the ground and trampled on. Soldiers, using the butt-end of their spears, drove their way into the crowd. A man, red with apparent fury, yelled 'Crucify him! Crucify him!' The soldiers ignored this provocation, but seized and beat unconscious a Galilean who had turned to strike the fellow.

The Procurator had lost some of his confidence. He said again that Jesus had done nothing that demanded sentence of death, but he was clearly worried. If there was serious rioting now, he would find it difficult to deny all responsibility for it. The Council and the crowd between them had driven him into an awkward position, and the people, because their priestly faction was far more active than the others, seemed to be growing steadily more hostile.

Pilate called for silence, and from the foreshore of the crowd the tumult ebbed away and left a strip of quiet. He would have Jesus flogged, he said, and then, because the Passover was a time of mercy and it was

135

usual then to set free some chosen prisoner, he had better be released.

The front of the crowd was well organized, and his answer was a howl of protest. Someone cried, 'Give us Barabbas!' and because many knew the name, and there was bitter insult in this alternative, the cry was magnified and many times repeated. Pilate grew angry, and spoke to the officer who stood beside him. With a clattering precision that could be heard above the yelling crowd, his Roman Guard sprang to attention, and advancing ten paces drove the crowd before them.

'Too many of your people,' he said to Annas, 'have had no breakfast this morning. I dislike their breath.'

'They're putting it to good use.'

'I suppose they're doing what you told them to do?'

'They're showing their loyalty to Caesar, and their determination to resist any faction or person who tries to usurp his power.'

Pilate frowned, and he answered harshly: 'I am Caesar's representative here, and I alone am responsible for the maintenance of his authority. I have never felt any need or desire to call on the people of Jerusalem for help.'

Too angry to be careful of what he said, Annas replied, 'If you release this man, you are no friend of Caesar's. He has called himself the King of the Jews, and anyone who calls himself a king is setting himself up against Caesar.'

The shouting began again: 'Crucify him, crucify!' Yet the great majority of the people had till a few hours before put all their trust in Jesus, heard him with glowing hearts when he taught in the Temple, and rejoiced in him. They had thought in the solitude of their minds: Here is my leader. They had told their neighbours: This is the man for us. He had made them glad, and they had determined to follow him wherever he might lead. But now they were bewildered, and could think of nothing to do but quarrel wretchedly among themselves, and cover their heads when the soldiers came. They had been taken by surprise, and they were perplexed by the strong and vociferous hatred of the minority scattered among them. They had no leaders. The Disciples had fled, none knew where. No one gave them encouragement, and their hearts contracted. They listened dismally to the shouting, ashamed and miserable, and though no more than one in five cried 'Crucify him!' the blood-cry beat its wings above them all.

Pilate, with grim disliking, had given in. A bellow of truculent applause greeted Barabbas when a warder brought him out and took the handcuffs from his wrists. Then those in the front of the crowd saw Jesus, still in purple, crowned by a Roman soldier with a circlet of thorns, and the troops turning into column. Like a great snake, huddled in its coils, that wakes and writhes slowly into movement, the multitude dissolved and gradually took shape anew as a long tail following their rejected King and his ribald escort. They turned westward through the city, to the Ephraim Gate, and towards a field broken with outcrop of rock, called Golgotha.

2

Judas was alone in the house. Barak and the other servants were somewhere in the crowd that followed Jesus to the palace of the Tetrarch, to the Praetorium again, and now to Golgotha. And Tamar and Cyborea were at the Procurator's, the guests of Claudia, Pilate's wife. She was a lady of unstable

137

enthusiasm, a great supporter of new religions, and she had recently been attracted to the teaching of Jesus.

Late the night before a young officer from Pilate's household had arrived with the offer of hospitality, and Claudia's urgent wish that they accept it. There was danger of rioting, he said, and there was some reason to suppose their house might be attacked. He did not explain that Claudia, who knew the Iscariot family well enough, had suddenly come to the conclusion that Tamar and Cyborea must be, like Judas, adherents of Jesus, though too discreet to make a parade of their devotion. He did, however, persuade them to accept the invitation. They were touched and a little flattered by its kindness, and not unaware of the case for prudence. They took their jewellery with them, and left Barak in charge of the house.

Barak was much alarmed when, in the small hours of the night, he heard a hammering at the door. He would not open it for some time, though Judas was shouting for admission. But his voice was unfamiliar, and so was his demeanour when Barak at last found the courage to let him in. Neither he nor anyone else had ever seen Judas drunk, but Barak could think of no other explanation for his condition now. Heavy drinking, tippling beyond all decent measure, must be the cause of that wild and helpless look.

Barak followed him upstairs and put him to bed without protest or resistance. He was puzzled by the fact that Judas did not smell of drink, but went no further to solving the mystery than to shake his head over it. In the morning, when news came that Jesus had been arrested, and all the other servants ran out to see what was happening, Barak went into his master's room and found him sleeping. Then he also left the house and hurried to the Praetorium.

When Judas woke he lay for a little while conscious only of relief. He was awake, and the room was full of light. He had been dreaming, of what he could not remember, but the nexus of the dream was darkness, and he had been struggling to escape. Daylight, for a little while, was mercy enough, and he took from it a sensuous brief happiness.

Then memory came back of his intolerable humiliation. He heard again the voice of Annas, killing his claims and cropping his pretensions. It was like a knife that cut his comb to the scalp, that lopped every branch in whose bright livery he had clad himself, and left him wintershorn, a naked stump. He turned on his bed, twisting to evade the echoed words, but the voice pursued him.

He resorted to a trick he had often used in boyhood, when memories of shame or embarrassment had been like invisible witnesses that described with icy reiteration the pitiable figure he had cut the day before. Then he had been used to shout them down by telling loudly, with repetition, whatever trivial thing he was doing at the moment ... 'Walking along, walking along, turning a corner, going downhill, now I'm hurrying, now I'm hurrying!' Louder and louder till memory was overborne : 'Hurrying, hurrying, I see a man, I see another, there's a man and there's his brother.'

He got up and dressed himself, and defied the witnesses with a gabbling commentary on his toilet. With a tale of nothing, told in a dull high voice, he kept memory at bay. But then with confusion he thought that someone might be listening to him. He went out, and through the house, and found no one there. He was surprised, but not alarmed. He supposed that something unusual must have happened, but he did not trouble to think what. He could not be bothered with speculation. He had enough to do to keep himself from thinking of Annas and repicturing his humliation.

The empty house was strangely fascinating. The rooms had a new and more decided shape, the courtyard with it flowering tree was quieter than a desert island. It was a secret place, a kingdom within walls and roofed by the blue sky that the tree supported on its coloured boughs. There were birds about the flowers, but except for the chattering of their small thin voices as they spoke among the leaves the court was silent as a well. It was delicious to walk in such a guarded silence.

He went into his sister's room, and smelt her familiar perfume. But it did not offend him. This was another province of his empire, where santal grew, and close and cassia. There were little jars of alabaster on the table, and the Ghiordes carpet hung upon a wall, a mystery of dull red, pale straw, and olive-green geometry. His mother's room was more richly furnished, and smelt of camphor. There was a cedar chest full of unfashioned silks in it.

He went into the servants' quarters, where he had never been since he was a child, and remembered the odorous dark corner where a kitchen-boy slept. He had subjects of many kinds, and Barak was his procurator. In Barak's room, a mere closet, there was a painted chest, and a twig from the courtyard tree was stuck in a red earthenware bowl that stood upon it. Beside the bowl lay a flute. He had forgotten that Barak played the flute. His house was full of unsuspected riches, and he was delighted with his exploration.

In the kitchen he cut a wedge from a cake of figs, and from there went on to the roof. The city was hidden by a ridge of houses, but on the other side, over the Old Wall, he could see a bright expanse of country, little fields and jutting rock, and the trees that guarded a narrow stream. It was the courtyard, however, that really delighted him. Looking down upon it, it was like a pool in the mountains, full of the milk-white light of dawn, and the tree with its red blossoms grew from the stillness like a strange and gorgeous weed. If everyone had run away from the house, scattered by some mysterious dread, and none ever returned, he could live at peace, alone, delighting in his kingdom, with never a thought for the tragic and tiresome and manifold busyness of humankind . . .

He heard a light knocking on the outer door. A hurried and impatient knocking, that stopped for a few seconds and then began again. He went down, reluctantly, and found Tamar standing there.

'Judas!' she exclaimed. 'They're going to kill him!'

He felt a savage resentment against this invasion of his peace, and his heart like a deep drum began to beat its warning. He put off the recognition of calamity as long as he could, pretending he did not understand. 'Who?' he asked. 'Who is going to be killed?'

'Jesus,' she cried. 'Jesus. They've taken him away. They're going to crucify him. I saw them all, the soldiers and the crowd. Judas, you must do something. You must stop them. The people don't want him to be killed, but they've got no leaders. They're frightened and they don't know what to do. The Disciples have gone, nobody can find them, and he's all alone. Oh, can't you do something?'

'When did you see him? Where are they taking him?'

'I came as quickly as I could, but I had to wait till the crowd had gone. The square was so full of people I couldn't move. They're taking him to Golgotha.'

Judas shut the door and came back into the courtyard. Tamar followed him.

'It's too late,' he said.

His thudding heart had drawn the blood from his brain, and he felt in his head a hollow vertigo in which his voice sounded like a pebble rattling in a skull. He struggled to control himself, for suddenly he realized there was something he must do. Something of the utmost importance that he must do immediately. Not the rescue of Jesus. It was too late for that, and he dared not face an angry crowd, nor even think of it. But something for his own sake.

Tamar was leaning against the wall, her head awry, exhausted. He backed away, moving slow and furtively. He knew now what it was, and if he could escape from Tamar it might be done quickly enough. He had almost reached the inner door when she looked up and cried in a querulous voice, 'Where are you going?'

'Stay there!' he shouted. 'I'm coming back. I'll be back in a minute.'

He hurried to his room, and in the coat he had worn the day before found the thirty pieces of silver. He must get rid of them. They were evidence against him. If Jesus was crucified, then this money made him an accessory to the crime. He would be guilty of murder, and that must not be. But if he returned the money, he would be washing his hands of the whole affair. He would have nothing to do with it,

142

and no tie would remain between him and the Sanhedrin. It would show Annas what he thought of him,
to throw the money in his face.

He found a purse for the silver, and put it in his
pocket. Tamar had gone to her own room. He crept
past her door, and out of the house.

Jerusalem was like a city desolated by plague.
The sun glared on empty streets, on windows un-
shuttered and shops where the shutters hung half-
open. A countryman's staff lay on the roadway, and
there a torn cloak. A dead man was huddled on a
doorstep beside a pool of blood. Two or three
figures hurried furtively round a corner, and a
lost child was crying in the street. As if it saw ghosts,
or the moon hiding behind the sun, a dog howled at
the staring sky.

The palace of the High Priest was deserted like the
city, but in a room in the Treasury Judas found the
elderly short-sighted man whom he had seen with
Annas. The old man was aimlessly busy, and fretful
about the disturbance of routine. He did not recognize Judas at first, and grew rather nervous when
he did.

Judas said loudly, 'Here is the money. You must
take it back.'

'Why do you say that?'

'There has been a mistake.'

The old man untied the purse and counted the
coins. 'This is the sum we paid you last night?'

'It was a mistake,' said Judas. 'I had nothing to
do with the matter, and I never asked for payment.
Annas was wrong. You must take the money back?'

'I can't do that,' said the old man. 'Not without
authority. You see, I entered the payment, and it
would put my books out——'

'Then cross out the payment! Take the money and cross it out!'

'No, no. I couldn't possibly do that unless I was specially instructed to do so, and even then it would mean a great deal of trouble.'

'But listen. This is an exceptional case——'

'And that is why I must refuse to deal with it. Exceptional cases always cause a lot of trouble, and you see I have no authority——'

'There's your authority!' shouted Judas, and threw the money on the floor. 'Now do what you like. I'm finished, I wash my hands of it. You can't touch me after this, I'm free, I had nothing to do with it. Do you understand? I had nothing to do with it?'

3

The three crosses stood in the sunlight, guarded by a company of Roman soldiers. On all sides there was unceasing movement in the crowd as those in the rear thrust forward, and those in front, shame-faced, let themselves be pushed out of the way; but here and there were islands of immobile mourners who sat on the rocky ground, their heads covered, careless of the feet that stumbled against them and of their restless neighbours. Many were waiting for the general doom that now they thought was inevitable, having neither strength nor desire to escape it. But on all the roads from Jerusalem were others hurrying in fear from the threatened city. The soldiers looked outward from the cross with scornful or speculative eyes.

On the southern boundary of the field, where the multitude was more sparsely gathered, three men were talking in a little coign of level ground that was walled on one side by a weathered ledge of rock. Since early morning they had been jostled in the crowd. They had fought their way to within arm's length of the Roman guard to see the crucified, and now they had struggled out of the throng and were resting. They mopped their sweaty faces, and sat on the ledge of rock, and chatted comfortably. They were little used to such a strenuous morning, for they were prosperous citizens, well-fleshed, and fond of ease.

One said : 'Well, that's over, and a good thing too.'

'A very good thing indeed,' said another.

'A couple of days ago,' said the third, 'when the outlook was so very uncertain, I was seriously thinking of selling my business for anything it would fetch and taking my family to Egypt.'

'Annas did well,' said the first. 'We've got to thank Annas for avoiding what would have been national disaster.'

'I blame the Sanhedrin. They've been far too lenient in the past.'

'It's a pity Herod isn't like Annas. They certainly need a firmer hand in Galilee.'

'Galilee's always the same.'

'He was a mischief-maker, pure and simple. I said so three years ago, when he started his campaign.'

'There's too much latitude in this country, and too much loose talking. He should have been stopped long ago.'

'Well, he's been stopped now.'

'They're all alike, these so-called idealists. They begin by inventing some new religion, and finish up by attacking property. And that's where they make a mistake, for though they get the ear of the rabble, they alienate all responsible people.'

'The real reason for the collapse of rebellion was that nobody wanted war. Or nobody but a few hotheads. Especially war for such a nonsensical cause.'

'People are beginning to realize that war solves nothing.'

'On the whole, I think, we can say that Jerusalem has come out of the crisis with great credit.'

'We ought to congratulate ourselves on showing, collectively, a great deal of common sense.'

'There was no panic to speak of.'

'No, people kept their heads remarkably well. For a while, of course, things did look bad, and I don't mind admitting that I took certain steps to safeguard myself in the event of further complications. I rather regret them now—I've probably lost a bit of money—but I'm not grumbling.'

'We have certainly no cause to be ashamed.'

'None whatever.'

'Thank heaven we had some realists on the Council.'

'Well, I'm very glad it's all safely over.'

'We all are.'

'Now we can get back to business.'

'Back to business . . .'

They got up and began leisurely to walk towards the city. But they had gone no more than half a dozen yards when a wild shouting behind them attracted their attention, and looking round they saw a tall and burly man, his black head bare to the sun, who was struggling desperately with a couple of soldiers. His face was cut and bleeding, but he was making a good fight.

'Barabbas,' said one.

'He'll be in gaol again by tonight,' said another.

After his release a number of his friends had taken Barabbas to a tavern. He had drunk a good deal, and then, leaving his companions, gone to Golgotha. He had struggled through the crowd, and seen Jesus on the cross. And then, for no apparent reason, he had turned and smashed his fist into the face of a man peering round his shoulder. Someone tried to hold him, but Barabbas threw him off, and kicked a fellow in the ribs who had fled too hurriedly, tripped and fallen. The nearer crowd drew back, and Barabbas, roaring in a wordless anger, ran amuck. A dozen fell bruised and bleeding before him.

Ordered to arrest him, two legionaries of the guard followed, and one wounded him on the forehead. But Barabbas disarmed him, came to grips, and hurled him against his mate. He might have escaped, but he saw a couple of Temple soldiers, and bare-handed assaulted them. He had nearly got the better of them when others came to their rescue. They overpowered him and led him away, half-dead, once more a prisoner.

4

It was nearly noon when Judas came home again. His feeling of relief, of freedom regained by giving back the price of betrayal, had made him restless and let him find a hazardous inconstant pleasure in walking about the almost deserted streets of the city. The death of Jesus did not worry him, for his mind was still occupied by the swollen figure of himself. He had filled his consciousness so full of his own self—his affairs and dangers and prospects and feelings—that like an eclipsing moon it covered the whole source of the sun save a bright thread of circumference, that shone with unnatural heat. He was alone in his importance, and had no complaint against solitude. When Tamar had told him that Jesus was condemned his heart had drummed a warning of the huge world that lay hid in shadow, and whose reappearance would put out his light; but he had soon forgotten it.

It was a blind man who again reminded him of reality. A blind man who tapped the pavement with his stick, and put his hand to unfamiliar walls, and cried for help. He had come out of his own territory, and was lost. Like a beast on moving sand, he felt for security but could not find it, and drew back trembling. His quavering voice called wildly, but the street was empty. Judas on silent feet went by and left him, for the frosty fear had touched him that if he gave the mendicant his hand, he would clutch it and never let go. But he looked back and saw the sightless man tapping and crying, and suddenly remembered that other beggar who had cried, 'Hail, the Son of David!' and the man at Bethsaida whose opening eyes had seen those about him like trees walking. He remembered Jesus.

He tried to put memory away, but now it held him fast. It lay on him like a burden, and his steps grew slower beneath the weight he carried. Now the desolation of the streets appalled him, and he saw Jerusalem as if it were a city taken in its sleep and slain before morning. He remembered the wrath of Jesus in the Temple, and his teaching on the northern hills where the wind blew keenly and the words took wing beneath a tall bright sky. The vast rotundity of the world was rolling into sight again, and his own light grew sick and faltered. He remembered his faith, and loss of it, and the emptiness of the city was like a pit that waited for his sightless steps. He found a staff on the road, that someone had thrown away, and took it for comfort.

The outer door of his house was open. He went in and found Tamar in a room darkened against the sun. She was sitting on a couch with her hands folded in her lap and a look of misery like a mask on her face. He stood in the doorway and for nearly a minute neither spoke.

Then Tamar in a lifeless voice said, 'You betrayed him, Judas.'

'Hush!' he cried. 'You daren't say that!' And looked fearfully over his shoulder.

'There's no one else here.'

'But it isn't true.'

'Are you sure?'

The words came wildly from him: 'It was to help him, to save his life. You don't know all that was going on. There were plots against him, and when war started we would all have been murdered. But Phanuel said that if he could be taken quietly and put in prison, no harm would come to him, and there would be no fear of war.'

'Phanuel told you that?'

'Yes!'

'And you believed him?'

'Why shouldn't I?'

'You weren't deceived by Phanuel to begin with. When did you give in to him? After that morning when Mary of Magdala came to see Jesus in Bethany?'

Her voice and manner were like his mother's now . . . In boyhood his mother had driven him from story and explanation with just such a cold remorseless questioning. She had taken pleasure in stripping him of childish pretences, in forcing him to full confession of inoffensive fraud and youth's white lies. She had liked to show her power, and believed there was virtue in humiliating him. Till he grew up he had always been frightened of her; not so much of her actual reproof, to which he had grown accustomed, as of some never-seen reserve of anger that might be in her. And Tamar was like her mother. They were both stronger than he. They would never understand, and so they would condemn him utterly.

'You loved him,' said Tamar, 'and you betrayed him. You told mother he was the only living creature you had ever really loved. You hurt her more than you can imagine; but that's not the point. You loved Jesus, and yet you betrayed him. That's what I can't understand.'

'There was a reason.'

'What was it?'

'You must let me think. There was a good reason, there was more than one . . . What did they do to him?'

'Crucified him.'

'Were you there?'

'You know I wasn't! I came here to ask if there was nothing you could do to save him. And you ran away.'

'I had business of my own.'

'What?'

'You can't understand.'

'Have you seen Phanuel?'

'No, no! I never want to see him again. I've got nothing to do with Phanuel, nor Annas, nor anyone. I wash my hands of them all. They wanted to bribe me, but they couldn't. That's why I went out this morning, to give back the money they offered me.'

'You had taken their money?'

'No, I gave it back, I tell you! Every penny of it.'

'You sold him!'

'That's a lie, the hell-heart of every lie in the

world! They tried to trap me, but I was too much for them.'

'Oh, Judas!'

'I tell you my hands are clean!' he shouted. 'I did what I did because I had to. Not for money. All the money in the world couldn't have paid for what I did. You say I loved him, and that's true. Truer than you think. Because I loved him as a child loves anything that gives it life. No one had ever given me such life before. He gave me peace of heart. I found peace in doing whatever he wanted, in believing his words. Till he began to change—and he did change! He said, long ago, that he had not come to bring peace but a sword; but I didn't believe him. No one could believe him when he said that. He would not break a bruised reed. He had said, Blessed are the peace-makers, Blessed are the meek, Blessed are those who hunger and thirst for goodness. He had no need for swords. But then I saw it was true, and he was going to set a man against his father, and make his household his enemies. And that was not peace, but war and death. And how could I love death and the teaching of death? I saw his face through the harlot's hair, and that was vile. I saw him scattering money on the floors of the Temple, and that was destruction. I saw a man killed, with a knife in his belly, and that could have happened to us all. So I gave him up, and I saved the people from death. I gave him up, though I loved him, and I saved the life of all the people of the city.'

His face had become gaunt and older than his years, and its pallor was like cotton-grass against his loose red hair. But his vehemence simulated strength —a brittle and precarious strength—and his carriage was not without dignity.

Tamar, with hardly a movement, still sat and watched him. She was nearly as pale as he was, but her swollen eyelids were red, her mouth was tortured and vindictive.

'You gave him up,' she said, 'to save your own life, not the life of the people.'

'That's not true . . .'

His mind played him false, and he did not know whether it was true or not. He felt himself shaken by conflict, but desperately repeated, 'It isn't true. But nothing I can say will make you believe me. Neither you nor mother have ever understood me or really believed in me.'

'You betrayed him,' she said again, 'because you were afraid for your own life, afraid of what was going to happen to your property . . . And what a fool you were! Because on your own admission he was the only one who ever gave you peace of heart, and peace of heart is the only peace there is.—There's no peace in the world.—And peace is what you want, it's all you want. But now you have betrayed him, and he is dead, and you have nothing left. You fool. You fool!'

She got up and stood for a moment, distraught, ungainly to look at, her arms raised as though the muscles against her will had contracted and drawn them up. And then in a sudden thaw her hardness melted, and she ran to the door, weeping. She turned, her face convulsed with grief, and cried, 'For thousands and thousands there is nothing left. To thousands of people he was their all-in-all, and you have robbed them. We have nothing left, nothing at all.'

Judas followed her out of the house, and watched her fumbling at the door. He wanted to stop her from going, but he could think of nothing to say. She went down the road like a rook with a broken wing. He shut the door and came back into the courtyard.

He was alone again, and had the house to himself. But it no longer gave him the comfort he had taken from it in the morning. He went from room to room, and all their familiar furnishing was dead. A table had the cold touch of clay, and the carpet on Tamar's wall was like the torn page of a book, its writing washed by the rain. In the closet where Barak slept the flute on the painted chest was a broken branch, voiceless and without meaning. You have nothing left, she said. He was afraid to go into his own room, because he might be lying there, and would start up with hatred to see the fool who had thrown away his life.

There was nothing left, nothing but remorse and fear.

Tamar had spoken truth—not all the truth, before God not all—but a damnable phrase of it. He had been thinking of himself when he did it, his safety and his wealth, because he was a coward and always had been. He had been something more than a coward—blessed are they who hunger and thirst for goodness—his mouth had once been desert-dry for the water of goodness, but there was cowardice in him too, like an acid that melted all the rest, and in the fumes of dissolution rose lies and bewilderment. In the mist of his corruption, against the bare horizon where his world had been, he saw the giant shadow of his deeds, a wraith who murdered him and what he loved. Fear and remorse, two hands upon a single stalk, squeezed out his essence. 'Master!' he cried. 'Jesus, Jesus . . .'

He ran into the courtyard, and its walls enclosed him. It was like a tomb in the bowels of the earth, but too hot for burial. The heat of noon was unbearable in its close confinement. He threw off his coat and stood panting for breath. The tree grew upward, tall beyond seeing to the hideous brazen sun, and sucked all life from the lower air. Not a leaf was stirring, but a bird flew screeching from its branches. And the city beyond the walls was more fearful still, for it was full of his enemies who cried against him, You have robbed us of all that gave us hope and the desire to live, and we have nothing left. The fear from without met fear within.

He had pledged himself to Jesus, who was right and the source of right, and Jesus he had betrayed for a shadow that was the shadow of wrong. Now there was nothing in him but this shadow and a stretching fear; and the outer world was nothing but a fear with reaching hands, because he had played traitor to the saviour of the world. Fear from without and fear within, and nothing between but the dead shell of his life. There was one refuge left.

Tiptoe, with the fumbling hands of a blind man, he went into the house, to the servants' quarters, and by another door to the stable behind them. He found a rope, and dragging it in coils behind him came back to the courtyard. In boyhood he had often climbed the tree to where it divided into two strong branches and made a swinging seat among the leaves and wine-red flowers. He knew the way.

The bough bent and resurged as the weight fell on it. The whole tree was shaken, and all its branches lashed the sky as though a gale was blowing. Like coloured snow a shower of scattered blossom fell slowly to the ground.

SATURDAY

FROM daybreak there had been stridulous and creaking noises in the courtyard, as men sawed through the branches of the tree. It was reduced to a bare trunk from which protruded a few lopped boughs, and then from the walls re-echoed the thud of an axe. The smaller sounds of the double echo were like a bantering disparagement of the labourers' effort.

Phanuel came on to the veranda and looked down The tree was roped and ready to fall. They guided it to its place. There was a sharp, disarticulated, cracking noise, and with a couple of blows the axe divided the last pieces of splintered wood.

A discussion began as to what should be done next. Some of the men wanted to cut the tree into logs, but no one could remember what orders had been given.

Phanuel spoke to them : 'Leave it alone for the present. You can come back and cut it up later. Go away now.'

His ruddy face had lost some of its colour, his demeanor that was usually so taut with self-assurance now seemed ill-fitting, as though he had shrunk inside it. He watched the men go out, and then half-turning saw Cyborea. She came and stood beside him, and looked into the courtyard.

'Thank heaven that's finished,' she said. 'I couldn't get away from the noise.'

'Yes,' he said vaguely. 'It makes an extraordinary

155

difference, doesn't it? It seems a pity to have cut it down. It was a lovely tree.'

'One of us had to go. I couldn't live here with that beside me.'

'No, of course you couldn't. I see that. I'd probably have done the same myself. But a tree's a tree, and in that respect it's a pity to have destroyed it.'

They sat down.

Phanuel, ill-at-ease, said presently, 'And what are you going to do?'

'Do? What can I do but go on living till it pleases God that I should die?'

There was less visible change in Cyborea than in Phanuel, but her large complacency had become a protective hardness, her eyes were sunk and dark with shadow. Grief and the specific feeling of loss had as yet hardly become articulate in her. They were still obscured by a sensation of gross outrage.

'Time,' said Phanuel portentously, 'is the great healer.'

'That he should do it here. That he should come here to kill himself. I shall never forget that.'

'You mustn't read any such meaning as that into it. He was unbalanced, poor boy, he didn't know what he was doing. We mustn't altogether condemn him.'

'He never showed any consideration for my wishes, but I never thought he hated me.'

'Of course he didn't. That's a terrible thing to say. Terrible for yourself, and in a way terrible for Judas too. For his memory. He was over-wrought, he found life too much for him, and—well, there's not the slightest reason to suppose that he was actuated by any ill-feeling against you.'

'Then why did he do it here? In this house? Why did he do it at all? He had everything to make life
156

happy. A good name, a good home, all the money he was ever likely to need. He had everything that anyone could wish for.'

'Everything but the appetite, perhaps.'

'What do mean?'

'He hadn't enough appetite for life. To enjoy life you must take it as it is, as you and I have always done. The world isn't all it should be, but if you have a good appetite you don't mind the sour bits and a bad smell here and there. But Judas was too particular. He wanted to set the world to rights before he could sit down and enjoy it.'

'It was that man who ruined his life for him.'

'Jesus?'

'I never want to hear his name mentioned.'

'If Judas hadn't been what he was, he wouldn't have paid any attention to Jesus. But he always had the idea that things should be made better than they are—though how he persuaded himself that Jesus could make them better, I don't understand. He had too much of his father in him, and not enough of you.'

'This would never have happened if Simon had lived. Simon could have argued with him, and shown him the folly of believing that a common carpenter from Nazareth could change the world. I did my best, but Judas would never listen to me. Never!'

'If Simon had lived he would have let Judas go his own way, and for the same reason that Judas took his life. Because he was never master of his own mind. He neither had the strength to find a belief that suited him, and stick to it; nor the hardness to disbelieve. Simon was a good man, but weak. And so was Judas.'

'Judas never had the brains of his father.'

'I don't know. I think he had. But he had stronger, more unbalanced feelings than Simon, and they discounted his cleverness. I was very fond of the boy. I thought he would grow out of his silliness.

Cyborea, hesitating and then speaking with visible effort, asked, 'Do you think I was in any way to blame for what happened? Could I have done anything to prevent it?'

Phanuel, a husky tremor in his voice, answered, 'It is I who should be asking that question. But I know the answer. I blame myself bitterly for what I did. I put a burden on him that he wasn't fit to bear. I forced him to make a decision, and the effort was too much for him.'

'But it shouldn't have been too much! You talk as if he was the only man in the world who had ever had to make up his mind. He made up his mind without any distress, so far as I could see, when he decided to follow the Nazarene. But then he was thinking of his own pleasure. Now, when it was a question of duty, of duty to the government and to his own people, he broke down and left us this heritage of sorrow and disgrace. I can't forgive him, Phanuel. I can't forgive him.'

'You mustn't be so bitter.'

'I am bitter! I've been bitter for three years, as any mother would be who had seen her son desert his home, and make a ruin of his life, at the behest of a crazy illiterate carpenter who paraded the country like a mountebank to persuade bigger fools than himself that he was the Son of God. The Son of God! God knows what was in Judas's mind.'

'He won the confidence of more than Judas, my dear. He affected some of the most unlikely people. I thought yesterday that Pilate would refuse to commit him. Pilate, a shrewd ambitious Roman magistrate. It wasn't only policy that made him hesitate so long, though policy was his reason for not helping us to begin with. But in that last hour of argument—I thought it was never going to end—he was coming under the man's spell. I could see it plainly. And if Annas hadn't frightened him by reminding him of Caesar, heaven knows what would have happened.'

'Pilate is a Roman,' said Cyborea contemptuously. 'A self-made man, and like all self-made men gullible under his skin. His wife is worse than he is. I had to listen to her for an hour while she talked about the Nazarene, and when I told her that we had a prophet or a messiah in Judea every two or three years—and had had ever since I could remember—she said he was preaching a universal religion, and Judea was incapable of appreciating him.'

'They have a great gift of confidence, the Romans. But they make many mistakes.'

A little later Cyborea said dully, 'What is going to become of me, Phanuel? Simon is dead, and Judas is dead. How can I live alone?'

'You have Tamar.'

'Have I? I suppose I have. She has been behaving oddly for the last few days, and I thought she was catching the infection too. But I suppose it will pass off now. Yes, I have Tamar.'

'She will be a great comfort to you. A warm-hearted and sensible girl.'

'But it makes an uncomfortable house when a mother and her daughter grow old together.'

Phanuel got up to go. 'I shall come back this evening,' he said. 'And you can leave all arrangements to me, of course. Try not to worry too much. For a boy like Judas I suppose unhappiness was inevitable, and we mustn't complain because we have to share it. Think more kindly of him, and that will help you.'

As he was going out of the blank unshaded courtyard, he met Tamar coming in. She stopped and looked at him with an expression of hard and hostile triumph. He saw with a shock of curious apprehension how much she resembled Cyborea when Cyborea was young. The boldness of youth and her mother's resolute assurance.

She said, 'You're going to be defeated after all.'

'I assure you,' he answered, 'that there's very little left to feel it. I have no sensation of victory.'

'You think Jesus is dead, don't you? You think that you and the Council and Judas between you have killed him and made a finish of his gospel? But you're wrong. He's still alive. He's more alive than you and your confederates will ever be.'

'Alive? It isn't possible. He was dead within a few hours.'

'You're frightened by the mere thought of it!'

'I don't know what you're talking about.'

'He promised, before he was made captive, that he would come back. He knew what was going to happen to him, but he knew the spirit within him was immortal, and that's why he made no attempt to save himself. He told some of the Disciples, "I shall see you again, and your hearts will rejoice." So in spite of all your trouble you haven't done yourselves any good. He's coming back, and his gospel is real!'

'You can't believe rubbish like that!'

'*Believe* is a poor word. Judas believed, and then he betrayed Jesus and hanged himself. Belief isn't good enough for me. I know!'

'Your poor mother!' said Phanuel.